Death Rub

by

Ashantay Peters

Death Rub

Cover Art by *Diana Carlile*

The Wild Rose Press, Inc.
PO Box 708
Adams Basin, NY 14410-0708
Visit us at www.thewildrosepress.com

Publishing History
First Crimson Rose Edition, 2014
Print ISBN 978-1-62830-407-7
Digital ISBN 978-1-62830-408-4

Published in the United States of America

"My man'll drop his bimbo once he remembers who I am and what I can do for him." With that statement, her muscles actually loosened. A smidgen.

Rooting for the bimbo, I fantasized about the poor guy who obviously tried avoiding Miss Stuck-Up. He must be some kinda loser.

Even so, kissing up a bit wouldn't hurt. She'd be gone in less than twenty minutes; and after one more client, I'd be on my way home to a hot bath, a glass of red wine and later, promised phone sex with my yummy new man.

"I'm sure you're right." Maybe she couldn't loosen up, but I knew how, even though I still had doubts about dating a much younger, very sexy guy. For some reason, the almost seven years between us stuck in my craw, though it didn't bother my cutie.

"You bet I am. If I didn't have the get-together tonight, I'd wear my sexiest lingerie, ice a bottle of bubbly, and call him. Cam Darrow wouldn't know what hit him. The bimbo would be a distant memory five minutes after he got a look at me hot and ready."

What had she said? About Cam Darrow? My knees weakened, and not in a good way. I lifted my hands and stepped away from the table in a daze. The after-massage recommendations I gave all my customers came automatically. Session's end hadn't come too soon. Good thing, because my brain hit a speed bump.

Shoot. The mutual hour we'd just experienced would've been even more uncomfortable if she'd known that we also shared a boyfriend.

Cam was so dead.

Dedication

This is for my editor, Ally Robertson,
who believed in *Death Rub* more than I did.
Thanks a bunch!

Chapter One

"I think my boyfriend's two-timing me."

My high school nemesis lay on the massage table before me. She bunched her muscles. Why Nicole Polk had made an appointment with me when she wouldn't release control on or off the table remained beyond my understanding. But her check wouldn't bounce, and I needed the rent money for both my work and home. I'd learned the hard way that summer months are a slow business time, and this year proved no different.

I concentrated on her constricted neck muscles. "Uh huh."

"Why do men do that? Run around?"

Knowing the former prom queen, and current mayor's daughter, didn't want my opinion, I worked on releasing a knot in her upper back. If she called me every time she had a snit, I'd never worry about rent money again.

"It's not that he doesn't already have the best available woman on the market. Moi, of course. Ouch! Maggie, you're pushing too hard."

"Sorry." I lightened my touch. "Is this better?"

I took her non-answer as a positive.

"Don't you get tired standing all day, Maggie? I mean it's not like you use your valedictorian brain. It's been fifteen years since high school, but I hear more older women are attending college. You could still go, right?"

As if the bitch didn't know the reason I'd given up a full ride to Duke University. Dodging her question, I changed the subject. "Try relaxing. It'd help if you breathed deeply as I work."

She raised her surgically augmented chest from the table and turned her head. Her turquoise contacted eyes flashed with anger. "Don't tell me what to do. I know I'm tense. That's why I'm here. My regular masseuse cancelled last minute." She lay down. "I want to look my best for the get together at Sloane's Tavern tonight. You can never tell who'll show up. Especially with the reunion starting this Friday."

Nicole shifted under the sheet. "My active social life keeps me hopping. It's stressful juggling all my appointments while selling the most real estate in the county."

Dang. Why did this woman make me wish I could unleash lethal karate chops on her spine? Perhaps her bitchy tone, the one that ate at my eardrums, held the answer.

After a few silent minutes, I thought she'd calmed down. Obviously she'd been chewing her mental cud and wanted to spew it out.

"My man'll drop his bimbo once he remembers who I am and what I can do for him." With that statement, her muscles actually loosened. A smidgen.

Rooting for the bimbo, I fantasized about the poor guy who obviously tried avoiding Miss Stuck-Up. He must be some kinda loser.

Even so, kissing up a bit wouldn't hurt. She'd be gone in less than twenty minutes, and after one more client, I'd be on my way home to a hot bath, a glass of red wine, and later, promised phone sex with my yummy new man.

"I'm sure you're right." Maybe she couldn't loosen up, but I knew how, even though I still had doubts about dating a much younger, very sexy guy. For some reason, the almost seven years between us stuck in my craw, though it didn't bother my cutie.

"You bet I am. If I didn't have the get-together tonight, I'd wear my sexiest lingerie, ice a bottle of bubbly, and call him. Cam Darrow wouldn't know what hit him. The bimbo would be a distant memory five minutes after he got a look at me hot and ready."

What had she said? About Cam Darrow? My knees weakened, and not in a good way. I lifted my hands and stepped away from the table in a daze. The after-massage recommendations I gave all my customers came automatically. Session's end hadn't come too soon. Good thing, because my brain hit a speed bump.

Shoot. The mutual hour we'd just experienced would've been even more uncomfortable if she'd known that we also shared a boyfriend.

Cam was so dead.

****

I stumbled toward the front counter. Dolores Quick stopped my drunken snail-like progress with a question. "Is Nicole ready?"

Dolores and I graduated high school the same year, and she'd gone straight into the personal services field. She'd climbed the mani-pedi ladder and now owned the Lotus Spa, located in an old Victorian just off Main Street. She looked the part, with a svelte figure accessorized by immaculate grooming, short light brown hair, and a white cotton aesthetician's jacket over black slacks. She'd already slipped on her party shoes, a classy pair of black and white striped heels. The open toes showed off a new pedi featuring bright red polish.

"I just left the room. Give her another five minutes or so."

Dolores laughed, her capped teeth gleaming like a television star. "I won't hold my breath. She'll want to put on a new face." She swiveled in her chair. "Are you sure you can't meet up with some of the old gang? Travis said...uh, sorry." She ducked her head and inspected her fingernails.

My stomach dropped. Travis. Had returned. Shoot. That's why Nicole wanted to shine tonight.

Dolores cleared her throat. "Ah, I forgot. Clarice Dawkins came in early. She's your last client tonight, right? Why don't you use Liz's room and get started? Get out of here at a decent time for a change."

Still reeling from Cam's defection and the news my old boyfriend had returned to town, I shook myself before more bad memories kicked in. "I used Liz's room for Nicole." I hadn't wanted Nicole in my personal workspace. "My room's open for Clarice."

Dolores stood. "Maggie, don't let Nicole or Travis keep you away from our reunion. You'll have friends there. Good friends."

I smiled, but from her reaction, my expression likely resembled a zombie more than a live being. She opened her dorm-sized refrigerator and pulled out a bottle of white wine.

She wiggled the bottle. "By the time I finish my wine, Nicole will be ready and we'll be out of your hair." She poured a generous splash into her glass.

"Everyone else has left, so I'll lock the door on my way out. Get the dead bolt as usual, okay, hon?"

I nodded. Dolores obviously expected a good time ahead meeting "the gang." Like that crowd ever had time for me. Well, except Travis, but that had ended fifteen long years ago.

At least with Dolores waiting on Nicole I wouldn't have to show my unwanted, pretentious, oblivious client out. My boss would handle that chore.

I entered the reception area, a medium-sized room with comfortable chairs, serene art, and soft lighting. Clarice stood at the lone window with her back to me, studying a scene outside. Maybe having just left Nicole sparked my imagination but I noticed a striking resemblance. From the rear, Clarice could be taken for Nicole. She had light brown hair rather than Nicole's platinum blonde, but their build and postures matched.

Luckily, that's all they shared. Clarice differed from Nicole like The Village People's songs did from Frank Sinatra's crooning. I walked her back and left her to get settled on my table.

As I exited, the full import of what I'd heard from Nicole made my stomach rebel. I hurried for the bathroom. Stomach emptied of what little remained after a light lunch too many hours ago, I washed out my mouth and bathed my face with cool water.

Cam owed me an explanation, at the least. If I ever answered his calls again. Right now that didn't seem likely. He hadn't mentioned dating exclusively, and the news that he also saw Nicole hadn't flown across the Granville Falls uber-efficient gossip lines. Had she lied?

He'd said he couldn't come over tonight, but had

given me a promise of "smokin' phone sex." Cam had been patient with my skittishness about making love with him. But maybe that's because he'd be meeting my hated nemesis at Sloane's Tavern later.

Nicole and I were the two magnetic poles that never attracted. Either Cam had multiple personalities or I resembled Nicole more than I knew. Scary thought.

Those ideas neatly pigeonholed in my "I'll think about it later, maybe, or maybe not" mental folder, I squared my shoulders and headed for the bathroom door. "Get Clarice out and get home" played as my running litany. Followed with a mantra of "I need wine."

As a good luck charm, the litany partially worked. When I knocked on Liz's treatment room door and called, "Nicole?" no strident tones returned an answer. I entered and saw that she'd gone, leaving no tip and a rumpled mess of sheets and towels strewn across the room. Shoot.

Clarice waited. I'd clean up later.

Propping open the door and cracking a window for fresh air, I walked down the hall. I knocked and entered. Clarice lay on the table but didn't answer. Hmm. She had a quiet mood going.

My initial anger at being delayed from my Cabernet by Miss Stuck-Up's mess faded when Clarice still didn't respond to my call. The room's atmosphere felt heavy and she lay too still. The CD I'd left playing ended. An aromatic candle flickered, but didn't lighten the room's undertone.

I'd like to think I paid attention to the chills traversing my spine, but I didn't. I only knew that, as a student of the human body, something looked wrong.

The answer didn't become immediately clear. I moved closer.

My shaking hand touched her shoulder. "Clarice?" I prodded her when she didn't answer or move. That's when her lolling head told the tale.

Clarice Dawkins wouldn't speak with me or anyone else ever again.

Her broken neck guaranteed that.

****

I huddled against the wall outside my workspace and watched as Detective Dirk Johnson, accompanied by his partner Matt Pulaski, arrived. Dirk recently hooked up with my friend, Katie Sheridan, after she and our buddy Ginger Howe were involved with a murder at The Yoga Studio. I still hadn't figured out if Dirk or Katie had lucked out more.

I straightened and greeted them. "Dirk. Matt."

"Ms. Stewart."

His use of my last name caused shivers. Too official.

Dirk put his hand at the small of my back and ushered me toward the spa's nearby seating area. After we settled in he asked, "Maggie, what happened?"

Matt pulled out his notebook and pen, putting me on notice that even though I hadn't been read the Miranda, my statement would be used for determining innocence. Mine.

"Dirk, I don't know. I finished a massage, then saw that my last client, Clarice, had arrived. After I showed her into my room, I gave her privacy time. I also checked on my prior client, but she'd already left. Then I, uh, found Clarice." I swallowed hard.

"How long were you out of the room?"

"Um, I don't know. I guess ten minutes. I didn't feel well, so it may have been longer."

"Did you try reviving her? Touch her in any way?"

"Yes, I tapped her shoulder." I swallowed non-existent spit down a dry throat. "I didn't realize she'd died, at first."

The next few minutes were more a quiet discussion than an investigation. Dirk walked me through my actions with Clarice, but I have no memory of what I said. I watched for any hint of expression on his face. Nothing. Not when he heard my client and I were the only people in the spa. Not even when I told him I didn't normally work on Nicole.

"Maggie, the news is going viral. A story about murder in a spa? Nudity implied?" He shook his head. "I know you'd rather go home, but I need you at the station for a statement."

I stood and my knees buckled, sending me sinking right back into the chair. If my mom hadn't died of cancer years ago, she'd have expired again with this news. I'd have hated for her to hear my name entwined with a murder investigation. I wasn't happy about it myself.

Somehow I found the strength to nod, stand and walk out with the detectives. Right into a barrage of bright lights, shiny yellow tape, and shouted questions. Granville Falls, North Carolina, is a small city, but proximity to Charlotte made us part of the metropolitan beat.

We hurried for the car and moved off, leaving the cacophony behind. Blood pounded at my temples and I concentrated on a sequence of deep breaths designed to lower my blood pressure. The inhalations hadn't worked by the time we hit the cop shop two hours after I found Clarice, and a migraine moved into full swing.

Katie waited at the front desk in company with several officers, a tall coffee cup in her hand. Dirk reached for the beverage, but Katie handed it to me. The way she turned away from him told me—and probably Dirk—more than words.

She grasped my arm. "Sweetie, are you all right? I didn't believe the news stories so came down to see for myself. One reporter said you were arrested." She glared at Dirk. "That must be a mistake." Katie patted my shoulder. "If anyone had to die, it should have been Nicole. She causes trouble without even trying."

Katie faced Dirk. "Whoever killed Clarice screwed up. Clarice didn't have enemies. She's a sweetie. Was a sweetie. Nicole Polk on the other hand, is included on more kill lists than Osama bin Laden was."

"The reporter is wrong. We've made no arrests." Dirk sent a scowl toward the watching officers who ignored his nonverbal "scram" hint. He crossed his arms and moved between us. "Go home, Katie. You're messing with my investigation."

She opened her mouth then closed it. I saw the realization that they argued in front of his coworkers hit, and her jaw tighten.

Dirk said, "See you later, Katie."

"I'll make up the couch for you." I knew she hadn't addressed me. She turned, leaving me to the questionable mercies of her lover. Somehow I knew his co-workers guffaws wouldn't sweeten his temper.

As I watched Katie exit, a staggering drunk reeled in shouting. A young officer caught and directed the man to the booking desk. Before he could get the drunk steadied, two more officers struggled in, barely keeping a couple of spitfire women apart.

"I forgot it's a full moon. The action is just starting. Let's move."

He took my elbow and we walked into a largish room with six scarred desks crowded together. Straight wooden chairs sat beside each of the work areas. Florescent lighting laid a sick yellowish haze over the scene. The room simultaneously depressed and frightened me. I shivered thinking about the bodies that had inhabited the chairs and the crimes the people sitting there had committed. And I stood next in line for the hot seat.

Dirk pointed at the chair alongside his desk and settled into his well-worn and stained cloth seat. "Can I get you anything else besides the coffee?"

A box of doughnuts sat on an adjoining desk. Oily food on my stomach? I shook my head. "No thanks."

"So, Maggie, let's start at the beginning. Why were you alone in the building?"

He walked me through my statement, or rather, he asked a few questions and I babbled. The full moon rowdiness, my migraine, and impending shock suppressed my natural filters. If they'd asked me where I'd planned on burying Clarice's body, I'd have answered.

A small, cogent part of my brain reminded me to take my time and read the damn statement before I signed it. Did I listen? I'm not sure, but I remember affixing my name at the bottom of a typewritten page. If something bad came from that statement, I'd claim temporary insanity. It'd be true, too.

Granville Falls Police Station wasn't big. I could

hear shouted questions coming from down the hall and deduced that reporters had given up at the crime scene and moved here for answers.

Dirk placed his hand on my shoulder. "Don't worry. No one will spot you. We'll take you out the back."

The weight of his gesture stopped my shaking. I caught his warm green gaze. "What do I say to them? The reporters."

"Nothing. If you feel pressured, say "no comment.""

"How do I get home? I can go now, right?" The idea of calling a taxi loomed as almost more than I could handle.

"We brought you, we'll take you home."

"My car's at the spa."

"We'll have someone drop it at your home when we've finished with it."

I briefly wondered if they treated every crime almost-witness with the same courtesy. Maybe keeping me vehicle-less wasn't civility, at all. I exchanged the worries for dreams of a hot bath and an open bottle of wine. Arriving not necessarily in that order.

****

When Dirk dropped me off at home, he pointed at a white pickup truck with a company logo parked before my house. Cam. I assured Dirk I'd be fine and levered my stiff body from his car.

Cam jumped from his work vehicle and followed me to my door. I pretended I didn't see his hunk-o-licious self, but his hand on my arm ended my acting attempt. Besides, my security lamp's glow highlighted his tall, blond self just fine.

"I saw the news bulletin. Maggie, are you okay?"

The day's events had exhausted my physical strength, attention span, and patience. I rounded on Cam's six-foot plus frame. "As if you care, you jerk."

He stepped back, my virulent attack surprising both of us. "What do you mean? Of course I care. I thought we had...never mind."

"Yeah right." I winced when I heard my jeering tone but didn't back off. Nicole's voice referring to me as a bimbo played in my head. "Your *girlfriend* came in and lorded it over me today. Then a client died, I ran a media gauntlet, got hauled to the cop shop, and you show up at my house saying you care. Right. Like I can believe you." I turned my back and tried inserting my key into the lock. The operation took a few tries but the lock finally tumbled.

Cam moved closer, his hand warm on my upper arm. His voice didn't linger anywhere near that comfortable temperature. "What do you mean, *girlfriend?*" He crowded me against the door. "I don't date anyone but you."

"You don't?" If my voice had popped out sounding any higher, I'd think I'd inhaled helium. "Nicole Polk said you have a thing going." My gaze ran over his muscled chest, encased in a tight cotton shirt. "She called me your bimbo."

"That woman has bat shit for brains." He ran the fingers of one hand through his short, dark blond hair. "She came after me when my engagement fell through. I told her to get lost, but she didn't back off."

I guess my "you're so full of it" expression didn't hold the answer he'd wanted. Although I knew Cam's manners would preclude him from saying, "get lost" in a way Nicole would grasp, I still had doubts.

He put his hands on my shoulders, his puppy dog brown-eyed gaze fully on me. "I mean it, Maggie. I haven't been interested in seeing anyone again until you."

"But you're so much-—"

"Younger," he finished. "Yeah, a few years stand between us. I know. So what? You're still the woman for me."

Right. As if he'd turn down a spin in a classic Jaguar for a ride in my dilapidated Pinto. Metaphorically speaking.

He shook his head. "Shit. Why am I even talking?"

Cam put his hand on the back of my neck, pulled me closer and settled his lips over mine. He tasted like cinnamon with a piquant aftertaste of dark chocolate. His sandalwood soap added another scent layer. A musky odor all Cam's topped off the aromatic mix. I relaxed into his flavors and heat before Nicole's strident boasts echoed through my mind like a ghost's shriek. Although I'd found security in his arms, I pulled away.

"This isn't a good idea." I looked away, avoiding his gaze.

Cam's fingers tipped my face toward his in a gentle, yet firm grip. "What's wrong?"

"I'm exhausted." Truth? I didn't know if I could stop myself from ripping him a new one once I started exploring his ties to Nicole.

"So why don't you let me rub your feet? Or make you tea or something? We could jump in the shower together. I know a few ways for releasing tense muscles."

This familiar refrain almost had me smiling. Almost, until Nicole's face popped into mind. Even though my heart considered Cam my man, I'd been putting off having sex with him. You'd think a massage therapist would be more at ease with nudity, and I am. With everyone's but my own in bed with a younger man.

It's not that my body had sagged, but I'd regularly seen Cam riding his bike over homemade ramps at age nine. I'd been sixteen, riding with then boyfriend Travis in his car. Worse, I'd babysat for Cam one night. I still remembered the cute starship p.j.'s he'd worn. Those kinds of memories made thoughts of sex with him tough even though he'd left childhood and a spindly body far behind. Sometimes living in a small town truly sucked.

"Look, this isn't the best time, all right?" I cringed hearing my shrill tone. I'd never been any good at hiding my emotions, and tonight had been no exception.

He stepped away from me his back erect. "Fine." He released his grip on my chin. "I'll wait. Call me when you're ready for the truth about Nicole."

His hurt tone punched me in the gut. My thoughts spun. I wanted to run my fingers over his high cheekbones. Instead, I stepped away, turned and went into the house.

Nicole and I had never played well together. She'd made it her business to lure away any man I dated. Along with that history, another Realtor had sold my mother's home at below market value. Bereaved and needing money for my mom's medical bills, I'd taken what I could get, but I'd never been sure if the market really had been slow or if Nicole had stuck it to me, some way. After that, I'd stayed clear of her and her cronies with the exception of Dolores, knowing she and

I mixed like members of opposing political parties. I had the feeling she'd scheduled a massage with me to screw me, again. Her opportunities for emotional torture must have slowed down.

Unfortunately, her stated claim on him had been so clear, I questioned Cam's honesty. I had good reason for not trusting men given my romantic history and Nicole's poaching tendencies. Looked as though some things never changed.

Chapter Two

Persistent knocking sent me stumbling for the door. If the bright, unrelenting sunlight illuminating my living room gave an indication, dawn had welcomed the day hours before. When I opened the door, my stomach rumbled like a crack of thunder.

Dirk and Matt waited, and because they were smart, didn't comment on my stomach noises. Even so, I sensed nothing good would come of my answering the door in a shorty nightgown. I hoped they'd keep their wisecracks to themselves.

"Good morning," Dirk said.

"Arrgh." I turned and walked toward the kitchen, figuring they'd follow me like pigeons to torn bread. Had I been awake, I'd have been nervous. Instead, I used my brainpower for firing up the coffeemaker.

Ten minutes later, my nasal passages were filled with the reviving scent of fresh coffee and I'd traded in my skimpy nightwear for shorts and a sleeveless top. I sipped my java and sighed. "So why are you here?"

The detectives swallowed their coffee and in a synchronized move, placed their mugs on the table. Matt pulled out his notebook and a pen.

Dirk tapped his fingers against the tabletop. "Did Ms. Dawkins use you as a masseuse on a regular basis?"

"Yes. We had a standing weekly appointment." I

pushed my cooling mug away. Caffeine traveled my bloodstream, sparking my curious genes. "Is that all you wanted? You came over here to confirm what I told you yesterday?" Somehow I didn't think so.

Matt kept his head down, his pen poised over his notebook. Dirk leaned forward. "Can you elaborate on your relationship with Ms. Dawkins?"

"Relationship? We didn't have one. Well, I gave her massages. She paid me. Other than that, nothing."

"I'd like you to describe your past dealings with Ms. Dawkins."

"How far back do you want me to go? Come on, Dirk. We attended grade school together. Is that where you'd like me to start? Or did someone spill the beans on our high school days? We had adjoining lockers in junior and senior years."

He tapped two fingers on the table while watching me. "High school would be a good starting point."

I sat back. My thoughts spun like a gerbil on sugar overload. One persistent idea kept surfacing. "What did Nicole tell you? Or did she sic her daddy on your boss?"

Dirk sighed. "Maggie, your class reunion starts this Friday. You work at a spa owned by a former classmate. Another high school buddy came in for an unscheduled appointment right before a third got murdered. It doesn't take a genius to see a correlation."

Holy textbooks. Put that way, even my math-challenged brain added up the facts and arrived at the same answer. I began to feel like Carrie on prom night.

Dirk leaned forward. "So tell me. What do you know about Clarice Dawkins?"

I rubbed the top of my nose as I thought over his

question. Would he believe "not much"? Perhaps not, yet it was the truth. Clarice could have been the original model for a private person. No one knew anything that she didn't want known. And that said a lot for our little gossip-central town of Granville Falls. Rumors aren't just part of life here, they're an art form.

As I mentally debated, a decisive knock sounded even as the kitchen door flew open. A dark head of hair swung in before the person's face appeared, but I knew who had interrupted. So did Dirk, and he didn't look too happy, if the muscle jumping in his jaw gave an indication.

I jumped up. "Hey, Katie. Want some coffee?"

My friend's wide grin lit up the kitchen. "You bet!" She managed a surprised look. "Dirk. Matt. I didn't know you were here. I'm not interrupting am I?"

Dirk's eyes narrowed.

Matt kept his head down but I could see his shoulders shake and the corners of his mouth turn up.

Dirk's voice was soft, his tone hard. "You didn't see my car? The one you must have parked right beside?"

"That sedan is yours?"

He stood and offered me his hand. "Maggie. Please call if you have any thoughts about Ms. Dawkins or her possible enemies. Or if you remember anything at all about the case that you haven't already related."

Dirk faced Katie. "Remember what we talked about earlier. You need to stay out of this." The couple watched each other silently before Dirk turned and left the kitchen.

Matt winked at Katie, shook my hand and followed his partner out. I felt oddly deflated after they left, then realized the testosterone level dropped with their absence.

"So, Maggie, are you ready to rock and roll?"

"No way. I'm not getting between you and Dirk."

My friend shook her head. "You won't be getting between anyone. I just want to help."

"Yeah, right. And Dirk's parting growl counts as a love song."

She grinned. "Yeah. He's sweet that way."

I couldn't decide if I should laugh or sigh. Or both. I did neither. Instead, I felt sick at my stomach. "Katie, touching a dead Clarice is something I never want to experience again."

Her grin dropped and too late, I recalled her recent firsthand experience with murder. "Sorry, Katie. I didn't think."

In an uncharacteristic move, she pulled me into a hug. "I wish we didn't have this in common."

I roused myself and poured her a cup of coffee topped with whipped cream and a sprinkle of cocoa. Sitting at the table, we sipped and sat quietly for a few minutes.

Katie lowered her mug. "You know, the killer must be someone from our class."

"Were you eavesdropping? That's what Dirk thinks too."

"It's the only thing that makes sense. I vote Nicole."

Laughter bubbled in my chest. "She really is a bitch, but I don't think she killed Clarice."

"Why not? She was on the scene and she sure had motive. Though Clarice had just as much incentive for knocking off Nicole."

"She did?" My thoughts churned. Had I missed hearing the news reports, or worse, the rumors?

Katie sipped her coffee, milking the suspense of her gossip stash to the limit. She licked the whipped cream off her upper lip and leaned forward in her chair.

"The story is that Nicole put the moves on Clarice's husband." She tapped her fingers on the table. "I heard two different versions of what happened. One has Clarice kicking the SOB out of their house, and the other has him walking out. No one is sure what happened. You know Clarice."

I gulped java, ignoring the liquid's heat. "Wow." I hesitated. "That explains her cancelled future appointments. She told me last week that she planned an extended European trip. Said she'd leave right after the reunion."

"Really? Huh. Well, I hope Nicole did the deed and gets caught. That nasty piece of work belongs in jail for all the crap she's pulled." She slid a guilty look my way. "Now it's my turn for an apology."

"No worries. She and Travis hurt me in high school, yeah. History."

I gnawed my lip. Sure, Nicole poaching my first serious sweetheart didn't hurt anymore, but her plans for Cam could. Although I hadn't exactly lived a nun's life, Cam had been the first man I almost trusted in way too long. Since Travis.

"Maggie."

I pulled my attention back to my friend. "What?"

"I'm caught up at work today. Contrary to what Dirk thinks, I really came by to get you out of the house."

Of course. Katie never told anyone how she felt,

she showed her friends she cared.

"Let's go downtown. Do a little shopping." Katie's eyes lit up. "And, if we run into someone who's got the skinny on Nicole, well, I sure wouldn't turn and walk away."

Now that made sense. My friend never exercised unless necessary but somehow kept her muscles toned. Maybe Dirk helped with the last.

"I hear and I obey, oh great one."

She leaned back into her chair. A smug grin pasted to her face, she brushed her dark wavy hair from her forehead. "Better put on some makeup. We may see a certain tall, blonde, built someone."

I opened my mouth to argue, realized I'd lose and headed for the bathroom.

****

We found a parking place downtown, not difficult mid-morning during the week. Katie wouldn't tell me what she had planned, and I was too numb to care.

She led my unresisting self down the street and around the corner. When I realized where she headed, I dug in my heels. Well as much as I could given the concrete sidewalk.

"No." I shook my head just in case she hadn't noticed my abrupt halt. "No way can I afford this store."

We stood under the awning of Pierre's, the most expensive clothing store in town. Women drove from Charlotte, even from across the region to shop there. Their couture stock was that incredible.

Katie inclined her head toward me while appearing to study the window display. "Play along, okay? I heard Nicole plans on picking up her dress for the reunion sometime today. It needed alterations."

"A built-in push-up bra to show off her implants?" Had a twinge of guilt followed my comment? Nope. I didn't even feel bad about my snarky remark.

"Wouldn't be surprised."

"Okay. I promise I'll be good if we see her."

"Geez, I hope not. Let's go."

I reached into my purse and patted my wallet, apologizing that it wouldn't see the interior of this shop anytime soon. My debit card normally makes periodic appearances in stores with signs reading, "Close Out Sale. Everything Must Go." That wouldn't be the case today.

We walked in and I inhaled the store's rarified atmosphere. If money has a scent, this place reeked. The carpet reflected wealth with a deep, soft texture and muted celery green hue. Multi-level crown molding topped off cream-colored walls. Jewel-toned dresses decorated padded hangers, and every sales person looked like a runway model. And that's just the first twenty feet or so. After that, the store does a credit check before letting anyone walk further.

Katie ignored the looks thrown our way by staff and other customers. I ducked my head, pretending to study the merchandise. Every tag had a bunch of zeroes bringing up the rear. I stuck my hands in my pockets.

My friend approached the closest employee. "Is Fiona here? My boss sent me for her alterations."

A clerk who reminded me of someone I'd seen on the cover of a glossy fashion magazine pointed to a back corner. I figured they imported their clerks because none of them looked like local girls. An older woman, likely the manager, motioned to an underling.

Instead of letting us wander through the store alone, possibly tainting the merchandise with our presence, we were now accompanied by a disgruntled clerk. She wouldn't be making a commission off us. Hey, life sucks sometimes.

A young woman pushed her way through a set of heavy forest green drapes. Garment bags with the discreet Pierre's logo were carried in each hand. Her blond hair had been twisted and pinned up neatly. She carried a few more pounds than the clerk, so her face looked healthy but not fat. A smock covered her upper body, but the way she moved implied athleticism.

She hung the bags on a nearby rack and addressed the clerk. Her deep blue eyes held a twinkle. "You don't need to stay, Mallory. This transaction will take a few minutes."

We waited until the clerk left on her search for better-heeled customers.

"Katie, what brings you to this bastion of capitalistic extravagance?"

"Fiona, this is my friend Maggie."

The young woman didn't hide her scrutiny. "You're the one who found your client dead."

I gulped. "Yes."

She clasped both my hands in hers. "I'm sorry for you."

The simple words held a wealth of sincerity. I relaxed for the first time that day.

Katie stood with her back to the store. "What do you know about Clarice Dawkins?"

She pursed her lips. "The dead woman? Nothing. She didn't shop here." Fiona removed the pencil from behind her ear and searched a crowded desktop. "Or if she did shop here, she didn't need alterations."

Katie pretended to look through her purse. Keeping her voice pitched low she asked, "What about Nicole Polk?"

Fiona dropped her pencil. "The bee with an itch? How much time do you have? Wait, forget it. I have a trunk load of work and don't have weeks to give you."

Katie glanced at me and winked. "What have you heard?"

Fiona found her pencil and reached for a pad. She pretended to write. "Nicole's a busy beaver. Pun intended. A real Miss Hit-and-Run. She'd hooked some married guy but told a friend he moved like granite, so she went on the prowl. She had her eye on some construction dude with a great butt."

Katie grabbed my shoulder. A nearby mirror showed me the gesture looked casual but her grip felt not light and friendly but restraining.

"So she hadn't reeled in the new guy yet?"

Fiona shrugged. "Who knows? I heard that last week but she works faster than a horny teenage boy on espresso." She rubbed the bridge of her nose with a finger. "Strange, though. I remember she acted edgy at her last fitting. I almost stuck her a couple of times. She wouldn't stand still."

Katie leaned forward. "When did she come in for the fitting?"

"Two days ago."

I jumped in. "Did she say anything to make you think she had a problem? Do you think she faced trouble?"

Fiona hesitated. She raised her voice. "I'm sorry, but Mrs. Jones must have misunderstood. The alterations will be complete on Friday morning, as promised." In a lower tone she said, "No idea. Sorry."

I glanced in the mirror. The manager made her way toward us. She hadn't brought gendarmes, but she didn't appear to need any.

Katie picked up the lie. "I'm so sorry to bother you. I know how busy you must be with special orders right now. My apologies."

She turned and grabbed my elbow. Smiling at the manager, she said, "Bye-bye now." We maneuvered past her and didn't hesitate in our straight path toward the door.

Once outside and walking away, I took a deep breath. "Damn, Katie, why did you drag us in there?"

"Ginger said the last time she saw Clarice, she was wearing a dress from Pierre's. I thought Fiona might know her."

"That's why you asked her about Nicole?"

"Sure."

"So you didn't bring me here to learn Miss Hot-to-Trot put the moves on Cam, not the other way round."

"Moi?"

Her brown eyes held a guileless expression, but I knew better.

"Thanks, Katie. You are one special friend."

"Don't go all girly on me. I knew Fiona would have the skinny, that's all."

Right. Katie and Cam worked for the same company. She'd acted to help both her friends.

"So why do you think Nicole acted all antsy at her last fitting?

She slowed her pace. "I'm not sure and but wish Fiona knew more." She stopped at the curb and checked for traffic.

"Will you tell Dirk what we learned?"

Katie snorted. "We haven't learned anything. So Nicole had a case of nerves a few days ago. Big deal. We didn't learn anything about Clarice. No, I won't bother Dirk."

I thought Dirk wouldn't consider withholding possible clues a bother, but I didn't know him that well. He remained Katie's problem. Better her than me.

"Come on," she said. "We've got a date at the Chocolate Fix."

****

The Chocolate Fix had to be Heaven's alternate location on Earth. Mona, the owner, had put together a sweet little shop with round tables, wrought iron chairs and the best chocolate this side of the clouds. The store's aroma of freshly ground chocolate and coffee beans alone sent me into raptures. I drooled just thinking about walking in the store.

Ginger Howe waved from a table near the window. We picked up a plate of truffles to share, coffee for me, iced chocolate for Katie, and joined her.

After we revived ourselves with treats that angels wished they could eat, we started our confab. I recited what I remembered of finding Clarice. I felt a bit like Pavlov's dog, answering without thought the same questions I'd heard repeatedly since walking in on Clarice.

"Wow," Ginger said. "A locked room mystery."

"It's not really a locked room mystery," Katie replied. "Have you been in that building? Offices all over the damned place. Someone could have come in earlier in the day and waited for everyone but Maggie to leave. Then they snuck down to her space, killed Clarice and left. Besides, those old double hung windows aren't secure. Someone could have come and gone that way and never been seen, especially if they hid in the bushes."

"Maybe." Her tone doubtful, Ginger brushed her namesake hair from her forehead. "But I thought Dolores locked the outside door when she left? Doesn't she use a deadbolt?"

They both looked my way. "Dolores said she'd use the knob lock not the deadbolt, but I was in the back. Plus, I left a window cracked in Liz's massage room. Other than that, I don't know what got locked or when. You're the two solving this case."

Katie waggled her index finger in my face. "Giving up is not an option. We need facts to work with here."

I refrained from telling her she'd echoed her lover's words. No telling how she'd take that bit of news.

"Dolores wouldn't forget to lock her business," I said. "And Dolores, Nicole, and the receptionist were still there when Clarice arrived."

I shook my head and watched my friends' smiles turn south. "The receptionist always pushes in the lock when she goes but leaves the deadbolt for the last employee leaving. Using the deadbolt is a pain because it sticks. There is no alarm system."

Katie rubbed her hands together. "You told Dirk this, right? He's checking the office for evidence that someone hid out there?"

"I told him, and I think he planned checking with Dolores. He didn't seem too excited."

Her eyes narrowed. "Really. Karma's a bitch.

Maybe I won't be too excited, either, when Dirk gets home tonight."

Ginger laughed. "As if. All he has to do is blink those long eyelashes and you're toast."

Katie plopped her fist on her hip. "Hush up. He could be bugging us."

I jumped. Ginger put her hand on my arm and scowled at our friend. "Katie."

"Oh, sorry Maggie. I was joking." Katie tapped her lips with her forefinger. "You hadn't worked with Nicole before, right? And you used someone else's room? Why?"

I nodded and related Nicole's reason for booking with me. "I used Liz's room because she left for the weekend and offered it to me. Her space is bigger than mine, decorated better, and has an adjoining bath for her mud wrap clients. She's used my room, on occasion. We do favors for each other all the time." I took a deep breath, heat flooding my face.

"Truth is, I couldn't afford to turn down Nicole's business, but I also didn't want her in my workspace. I wanted her thinking I'm successful. You know, in demand." I shuddered. "I should have told her to get stuffed. Then Clarice might still be alive."

Katie shook her head. "I bet Miss Stuck-Up had an ulterior motive, something with you in mind. No doubt she heard you and Cam are an item and came in to heckle you."

An item? Crap. With or without a bed sheet tango, Cam and I both had reasons for keeping our budding relationship private. Too bad nothing remained secret for long in a small town. Not that we'd expected otherwise, but we'd hoped for more time under the radar.

Katie sipped her coffee before continuing. "Don't you think it's strange that Nicole was present at the murder scene? Especially given your mutual history? Her purpose for making an appointment with you had to be underhanded."

Ginger shifted in her chair. "Katie has a point. But besides Nicole's nasty tendencies, an unknown someone could have waited in an office then left through a window or even the front door. More possibilities exist than I thought."

Their idea of an intruder, potentially Clarice's hidden assassin, had given me hope. "I trust Dirk. The mayor's buddies are putting on the pressure but I'm not in jail. That says a lot for him. He could have taken the easy way and charged me with murder."

"Maybe I'll be nice to him after all," Katie said.

Ginger leaned close and whispered in my ear. "Never a question in my mind."

"Meanwhile, I'll make sure Dirk checks out our theories." Katie's grin left no doubt about her planned approach.

"I don't want you jeopardizing your relationship. Or putting yourself in a killer's path."

"Hey, Ginger and I are the Demonic Duo. We can handle it. Right, partner?"

Ginger nodded.

I wouldn't refuse their help. Last spring they'd faced down a killer and a blackmailer. If the two could get their ideas a hearing at the cop shop, I'd feel better.

Chapter Three

I tossed and turned all night, unsure whether I should phone Cam. Taking the easy way out, I dressed and dragged myself to work, leaving the call for later.

Dolores had called to say the spa would open as usual. Chances were good I'd have a full schedule—everyone knows murder scenes always attract the ghouls—and Granville Falls is no exception. I figured I'd be fending off questions as much as releasing tense muscles.

A varied selection of music seemed a requirement for facing the day I knew waited. I rifled through my CDs and picked out a dozen favorites. Tossing in a sheaf of sage for smudging my workspace, I left for the spa. Surprise, surprise. The client parking lot looked less than half full, but the day had just started. After parking in back, I grabbed my bag and hustled inside.

"Hey, Dolores. I didn't expect to see you so early." I figured she'd been contacted by the police last night, though her questioning likely hadn't taken as long as mine had. I avoided asking what time she'd finished making her statement.

Her movie star grade smile gleamed in the low lighting at the front desk. "Thought the crowd might get out of control without me here helping out."

To underscore her words, the phone rang. Dolores made a shooing motion with her hands and I followed her silent directive down the hall. A police officer had tucked one end of the crime scene tape under my nameplate beside the door. The sight robbed my breath. Part of me registered surprise the spa had been allowed to open so soon. Yesterday, the crime scene techs had been scurrying around, today, business as usual. Guess being close friends with the mayor's daughter didn't hurt, not that I complained. Bills would always be due, and being able to work counted as a blessing.

I returned to the desk. "Um, Dolores, where should I set up?" I paused. "Do I even have any clients?"

Her lips twisted into a sardonic smile. "You're kidding, right? Yes, you have clients, a full schedule as you've probably guessed. You know what this town is like, full of gossips and lookey-loos."

I nodded and stood still, feeling like a socially challenged teen.

"Liz said you should use her room. She's taking off a few more days."

I entered Liz's space and found the mess Nicole had left behind still waited for me. Good thing Liz hadn't come in. Her screams would reverberate until December.

Cleaning up the linens didn't take long. I could strip and remake a massage bed faster than a NASCAR driver finished a lap. Even though the cops had closed the window, the open door had done the trick for airing. Nicole's stale perfume on an empty stomach? No thanks.

Minutes later my first client, the town's biggest gossip, Mrs. Goode, appeared in the doorway. Lucky me.

Mrs. Goode was a short woman who made up for

her lack of physical stature with a mean spirit and big hair. Her circa 1960s hair style—teased and sprayed into strict obedience—left no doubt about her life's philosophy. She also had a bosom that I could only describe as "shelf-like." You know, the ones that jut out like the Titanic's prow? Luckily, or maybe not, she also doused herself with so much perfume, you could smell her coming. Right now I wanted to turn on a non-existent ceiling fan and open a window.

I offered her a towel for wrapping her hair.

"Thanks, but that's not necessary. I'm headed to the Hair Shack after we finish." She smiled. "It's my regular day there."

My stomach dropped. The beauty salon, A.K.A. the Share Shack, acted as Granville Falls' gossip central. Mrs. Goode's early morning appointment meant she wouldn't take a chance on being anything other than first with the "news."

Everything went smoothly considering I kept repeating that I had no information about the murder scene. Including Mrs. Goode, many of my clients were new, so I concentrated on learning their muscles. I figured after the murderer's arrest I wouldn't see them professionally again. But, ya never know.

I had a half hour break for lunch and munched an apple. Keeping busy with work hadn't helped a whole lot. Unflagging curiosity kept my attention wandering to my taped-off massage space.

Hoping human interaction would corral my thoughts I ambled to the front desk. "How does my schedule look for this afternoon?"

The receptionist pointed in the direction of Dolores's office. "Boss said she wants to see you."

My stomach dropped. This couldn't be good. Dolores looked up at my knock.

"Hey, sugar, come on in. And close the door."

My heart followed my stomach down to my toes. Dang.

"Maggie, I hate to do this, but I have to send you home."

"Why? Did the police tell you I couldn't be in the building?" That thought had me fighting mad. I'd call the police chief and scream.

"Sit down, Maggie."

I hadn't realized I still stood, and my clenched fists wouldn't inspire Dolores to trust my reactions. Sinking into the chair across from her, I folded my hands in my lap.

"You can be in the building. I checked with Dirk before calling you this morning."

"Then what? Why?"

Dolores looked at her hands. "We've had a number of cancellations. Your schedule has fallen apart."

I stared at Dolores, my hands now fisted. This scenario proved way different than I'd expected, especially given the prurient interest of my first clients. What would cause a bunch of gossipmongers to desert an unfolding story?

She looked up. "Why don't you head home? You look like you could use some rest."

Although she used a gentle tone, I figured she avoided giving me any kind of explanation. Moving from a packed schedule to nothing couldn't be coincidence.

My gentle tone matched hers. Almost. "Mind telling me if anyone gave a reason for canceling?"

Dolores needed to study her fingernails for the answer. "No one said."

The answer almost bowled me over. I knew she lied. That hurt, more than the cancellations adversely affecting my ability for making rent.

"Dolores, we go way back. I can't believe you aren't telling me the truth. Don't tell me these women think I killed Clarice."

Her quick reply told me the truth. "No, no that's not it." She sighed. "Look, someone is spreading stories. Not that you killed Clarice, though."

I hated that I had to pull the story from my friend, but the unexpected cancellations placed my livelihood at risk.

Dolores nibbled at her lower lip, a sure sign of her nerves. "You have to promise you didn't hear this from me, okay?"

I nodded. "One of your cancellations told me they'd heard your massage skills are um, lacking. That instead of feeling relaxed, they saw another therapist to work out the kinks you left."

Although most of the morning's clients were new, I'd done a good job. The women had all left with the noodle-legged gait of relaxed muscles. I'd gotten great tips. If one of my clients had been dissatisfied, I sure hadn't seen it.

I studied Dolores. She didn't meet my eyes as she shifted in her chair. My continued silence caused her hands to fidget. Something stunk at the Lotus Spa and not rotten cheese.

"It's Nicole, isn't it? She's saying something and scaring off the clients."

The muddy red color flushing my boss's cheeks

told the story without her saying a word.

"Damn it. Why?"

"Sweetie, I don't know that Nicole is behind the cancellations."

I narrowed my eyes and bit back a nasty word. "I get that she's your friend. You have my condolences." I stood and headed for the door then stopped and turned. "Will you at least level with me?"

Dolores sighed. "I owe you that much." She rubbed her hands together. "You know I trust you, but this is my business. I can't take chances."

After my mom died five years ago, I floundered for over a year, lost in grief. My college scholarship was long gone, and I'd lost my coping skills. Dolores took me under her wing, steered me into massage therapy and gave me a shot at building a client list. I owed her. Releasing a sigh of my own, I turned and sat in front of her. "I understand. Just tell me what you can, please."

"For whatever reason, Nicole wants to sink you." Her muttered next words almost escaped my ears. "I wish she'd give it up."

Give what up? Before I could ask, Dolores resumed a normal tone. I wondered if she knew her last comment had been made aloud or if she'd wanted to head me off.

"I think she's been hinting that the police are going to arrest you for Clarice's murder later today." She rubbed her arms. "I don't know for sure, and I can't say more. "

I understood what Dolores hadn't said. A word here, an implied threat there, and Nicole—or her father—could ruin business prospects, reputations, pending deals. Although as a town native I had plenty of friends and clients, few of them were as affluent as the newcomer country club set Dolores wooed and Nicole hung with. The ones who'd made up my now destroyed afternoon schedule. She'd sold the wives their McMansions and her daddy had attracted their husband's businesses with favorable tax deals. Nicole acted like a one-woman wrecking machine, someone who after a non-declared truce had again turned her sights on me.

My thoughts reeled. Her infamy made no sense, except that in a strange way, Nicole and I had been headed toward this showdown for years.

"You can see the problem, right?"

My stomach held lead. "Yes. I'm a liability."

Dolores reached for my hand. "Look, I think it's just that I have some nervous nellies. This situation will calm down and folks will forget. Once the murderer is caught—"

The blood drained from my face. My lips tingled like I'd gotten an overdose of Botox. Not that my naturally full lips needed the stuff. "Is Nicole saying I killed Clarice?"

"Nooo."

Riiight.

She stretched. "You know, Clarice's murder doesn't make sense. She was quiet, nice to everyone. Who'd want to kill her?"

"Not me. Adjoining lockers aside, we weren't close friends in school and it's been all business since she started coming to me for massage." I remembered Clarice standing at the window, her marked resemblance to Nicole.

Dolores watched me like a Border Collie in a field

of sheep. "You've remembered something. Or do you know who killed Clarice?"

I sure couldn't tell her. She'd just run to her friend, and I didn't want Dirk ticked off with me. Instead, I'd mull over my memory and only talk with Dirk if it felt right.

"No. I don't know who killed Clarice, just an unrelated something I remembered. Nothing important."

"We'll continue scheduling appointments for you."

Yeah. Like anyone would be booking once Nicole completed her hatchet job.

"Thanks, Dolores." I stood on shaky legs and wobbled to the door.

"Listen, if you need help you'll be sure and let me know, right?"

I nodded half-heartedly. Gathering my dirty linens, music and the sage that hadn't cleared the negative vibes after all, I plodded to my car. Now what?

****

The gods of negative coincidences and weird occurrences weren't done with me. I arrived home and saw a strange car in my drive with a man sitting in the slanted shadow of my porch swing. Stopping my car on the street, I squinted toward my house. Dang, my eyesight must have failed. Or perhaps I imagined seeing the boy who'd dumped me in high school, now turned man. Nope, no hallucination from the drugs I'd used once and swore never to touch again. Travis Knowles stood at the railing and waved. Shoot.

Against my better instincts I pulled in beside his car. Slamming my gearshift into park, I shut down the engine and sat, afraid to leave my car. Life hadn't treated me well lately, and fear had become my reluctant friend. Reluctant on my part, that is.

I took a deep breath, scrambled from the car, and forced a smile. "Travis. Long time." Those two words hung like the accusation I hadn't intended to voice.

Scanning him head to toe as I walked closer, I hoped he didn't notice my scrutiny. Dang, but he still looked good. Travis had retained a lean, muscular build. A tight black tee hugged his shoulders and lay flat over his abs. He wore his hair longer, but the gold and red highlights I'd always loved remained, picked out in an errant ray of sunlight. His appearance whispered he'd done very well for himself. I wondered why he'd bothered looking me up.

"Maggie." His voice had deepened, leaving a caress I must have imagined around my name. We stood watching each other, not really sure how to proceed after years of mistrust between us.

He cleared his throat. "Listen, I want to, um, apologize."

I didn't pretend a misunderstanding. I'd already had a crappy day and game playing lay beyond my capability. "Not necessary. Lots of years ago."

"Well, I do want to talk." He stepped off the porch, moving closer. "See, I was a rat bastard. I knew it at the time, but I dunno. Must've been too stupid and young and didn't know how to fix my mistake."

"Must have been" my ass. "Your hormones made you do it, right? Dumping me after two years and talking about a future together? For someone you knew would put out instead of waiting for me and marriage the way you promised. That your story?"

His face reddened but he didn't answer.

I snorted before I could stop myself. "So now you want to make nice, have me accept your apology and you can walk away with a clear conscience, right?"

"Well, yeah. I guess. I mean I'd like you at the reunion. You know. Like friends."

"Like friends."

"Uh huh."

Okie dokie then. My blast from the past just wanted to have fu-un.

"It's been a hard day and I've been working like a dog lately. Mind if we take this up at another time?"

"Sure, sure. Just, you know, think about coming to the reunion. Because it would be good if you were there. Kinda like old times."

Right. Just Travis, Nicole, and me. Gotta love it.

"I'll think about it. Thanks for stopping by, Travis."

"Yeah, well, I'll get out of your hair. Just wanted to stop by and say, you know, hello."

I crossed my arms, hugging myself. "Sure Travis. See ya."

I felt like a total idiot and at the same time, ticked off. Royally. Travis coming over and making nice? Who'd have thought?

"See ya." He stepped past me then halted. "And Maggie?"

I held still but met his eyes.

"I've missed you."

He moved away from me before I comprehended his words. He missed me? In what alternate dimension did I hear those words after the crappy day I'd experienced?

Travis jumped into his car and drove off. Then the

jokester who runs this universe pulled my other leg. Cam's work truck replaced Travis's car in my drive.

I debated about avoiding my young would-be lover just a moment too long. By the time I'd decided, Cam waited at the bottom of my stairs.

"Cam."

"Maggie."

We went through a silent stare routine.

"Who's the dipstick who just left?"

"An old friend. Not that it's any of your business. And why are you here in the middle of the day?"

"Shit, Mags. If you don't want me, just say so." He brushed his fingers over his short hair. "I couldn't wait any longer for your call."

Dang. He'd said he'd wait for me to phone, and I'd blown him off. Why? Why did he keep coming around? My confused thoughts must have flickered across my face because Cam shifted closer. I went on the offensive.

"Look, Cam, you're a young guy. Why don't you just move on? Find someone closer to your own age."

His lips tightened. "'Give it up, already. It's you I want."

"Really." My statement sounded like a question.

Cam's straight lipped mouth tipped into a tentative smile. "Really. No question in my mind."

He almost had me convinced. When in doubt, trot out the Southern hospitality. "You want a cold soda?"

Cam's lips curved up. "If I can stay while I drink it instead of having to leave so I can change out of wet clothes."

Dang, but I couldn't help myself. A grin broke out, and it sure felt good. "I wouldn't waste a good cola by tossing it at your head." I walked to my door then I looked over my shoulder at Cam waiting at the stair bottom. My gravelly voice gave away more than I intended. "So are you coming in?"

Two seconds later, his large hand at the small of my back became the only answer I needed.

Chapter Four

Attending the high school reunion had not figured in my plans. I could think of many better activities for a beautiful late-August weekend. That's what I'd told Dolores yesterday, Katie last night, and Cam this morning. In fact, I thought Clarice's murder a perfect reason for canceling everything out of respect.

No one listened. They said classmates had traveled and spent too much money to cancel the reunion. That was just the first argument in their railroad Maggie campaign. I could still feel the cold steel tracks on my back as they ran over me one by one. I'd tried ducking out of Saturday's golf outing, the breakfast, and the fashion show luncheon saying I had clients. No luck. Dolores removed my excuses by announcing she'd rescheduled my appointments. Finally I agreed I'd attend tonight if they'd let me off the hook for the Saturday night sock hop. Even with the compromise, I didn't stop looking over my shoulder.

Truth? I'd been class valedictorian who'd earned a full scholarship to an eminent university. Now I struggled in a massage therapy practice. While I was proud of my profession, it was a far cry from the cancer research career I'd planned. I knew I'd be viewed as someone who hadn't lived up to her potential. I didn't look forward to the comments and looks I'd garner.

Tonight kicked off the reunion with a cocktail

mixer, dinner, and dancing. My mirror reflected a face I normally knew well, but I couldn't be sure I'd recognize myself without a nametag. And my hair and clothes? I appeared grown-up in a scary sort of way. My dark strawberry blonde hair had been smoothed into a twist with a few little curls at the temple courtesy of Dolores. She'd also shadowed my green eyes. But the dress that hugged my curves and made me look like a Hollywood red carpet stroller came from Ginger. She assured me Cam wouldn't know what hit him. I wasn't sure I knew what had hit *me*, and I'd been there for the renovations.

I figured the best part of wearing all this would be Cam stripping it off me later. A girl could hope. It's my middle name, after all. Really. Maggie Hope. Guess it could have been worse. My mother adored Rod Stewart—no family relation. If my dad hadn't protested, I'd be Maggie May. Yep. Think about that in connection with grade school boys for a few minutes.

Now I waited in my living room for my I'm-not-gonna-count-years-ever-again younger boyfriend. Yes, I'd decided life was too short to keep holding out on Cam and, more importantly, myself. Up to this point, we'd remained in the heavy petting stage. Cam's patience and attention hadn't flagged, and I'd finally grasped he liked me for me. Looking at my sexy reflection tonight made me realize I'd been wasting myself, drowning in fear of the unknown. Cam hadn't lied, but Nicole had. No way I'd let her screw me over again. I figured Cam would approve of my conclusion.

I tottered to answer the door when the doorbell chimed. Cam stood on the porch looking oh so luscious in a dark suit and charcoal-colored shirt teamed with a colorful blue and green necktie. Looking close, I noted small tropical fish within the swirls. On him the combo worked well. Getting lucky took on a whole new meaning. I sucked down excess saliva, happy I'd beaten down my fears.

"Wow. Smokin'." Cam's throat muscles worked but he didn't speak past his two-word greeting. He rubbed the nape of his neck and shifted. Still, he remained silent.

I took his silence as a good thing. "Come in."

He leaned against the doorframe, ankles crossed. "Honey, if I come in, we're not going out."

I brushed his lapels then slipped my hand under his jacket. His heart beat double time, another good sign. "Is that such a bad thing?"

Cam straightened, lightly encircling me with his arms.

Silently cheering that I'd have an excuse for missing an unlamented reunion gathering, I stepped into his embrace. "I've got popcorn and action movies." I paused long enough to see his pupils darken. "Some beer. Interested?"

He ran his hands over my bare back, resting one at the base of my spine. He bent and kissed me. Then I felt the corners of his mouth turn up against my lips. "Yes, but you're not getting out of this event tonight. I promised."

I pushed against his chest. He winced.

"Promised? Who? No, never mind." I blew a breath. "Dolores. Katie. Ginger. Pick one, but I'd guess all three."

He straightened, extending his hand but not answering. Smart man.

I grabbed the matching evening bag Ginger had lent me with the dress and closed my door behind us. My ingenious truancy plot had failed.

Cam wrapped his arms around me when we reached his vehicle. "Of course, I didn't say how long we'd stay, just that I'd get you there."

I smiled. Yep. Cam was my kind of guy.

He helped me in then circled around and slid behind the wheel. I put my hand on his muscled thigh. "For that kind of guarantee, you deserve the best I can give you."

He glanced at me. His hand stilled over the key. My expression must have telegraphed my resolve, because I saw a flare of passion spark his eyes. His throat moved. "Damn promises."

Cam's hand moved from the ignition and cradled my jaw. His lips moved over mine with slow assurance and heat. "We'll find your friends, let them see you showed, then get the hell out of there. I've got a lot of lovin' saved up for you."

My hands closed on his shoulders, pulling him closer. "We could take a selfie of us all dressed up and text the photo."

He nibbled off my remaining lipstick. "I'd love to check out those dress seams, hon, but I made a promise." We traded saliva for a few minutes.

Cam pulled back and rested his forehead against the steering wheel. He sat up, blew out a breath and reached for the ignition. "That's the last damn promise I'm making to your friends."

I looked out the side window and hoped he didn't see my smile reflected in the side mirror.

The valet took possession of Cam's car at the

Granville Falls Country Club entrance. Cam opened my door and assisted me from the vehicle. The entry—surrounded by white stucco, large pots of seasonal flowers, and impressive carriage-style lanterns—loomed before us. As we stepped onto the royal blue outdoor carpet, I sent up a small prayer asking that Nicole be far, far away when we registered inside.

Obviously, the high school reunion gods hadn't heard my plea. Or maybe they held a grudge against me. Nicole didn't show an ounce of mercy when she spotted Cam with his arm around my waist. Not that she had any compassion in her heart. No, it seemed more that if looks could kill, her slit turquoise eyes would have incinerated me into a pile of cinders yesterday.

"Maggie." Nicole reached for a "Hello, my name is" label and marker. I debated asking for a different tag given the way she'd mangled the one she extended. Didn't matter. What with my dress's low cut, I didn't have a place for a label anyway.

"Cam." His name hissed from between her clenched teeth. She slapped a nametag and pen on his open palm.

Okay then. We were on track for a wonderful evening. Good thing I had popcorn and movies at home. I knew I couldn't stomach Nicole on a tear for long.

Apparently Nicole realized she'd given her feelings away because her face morphed to gracious smile mode. Either that or she thought she could take Cam away. I voted for the latter given her successful track record with my boyfriends. "Have a good time you two."

We had turned from the table when a low purr sounded behind us. "Oh, and Cam?"

He looked back over his shoulder and I peeked around his side. Nicole sat forward, her boobs crowding her neckline. Apparently she took the term "little black dress" literally.

"You'll save me a dance later, won't you?"

Her voice cooed. My hackles rose as she sent me a sly glance.

"A slow one."

Cam cleared his throat. "I'm not much of a dancer."

Talk about a half-assed response. My brain teemed with put-downs I knew I wouldn't use.

My tense muscles under his hand must have notified Cam that he hadn't shut down Nicole strong enough.

"Besides," he said. "I'm not sure we'll be here long." He looked at me with a sexy smile slapped all over his face. "We've got private dance plans for later."

We strolled into the main room, and I held myself back from punching the air with a victorious fist. Woo-hoo. Finally, Nicole had gotten hers. I couldn't wait to share the news with Katie and Ginger.

I hugged Cam's waist tight, my other palm against his chest. "You deserve a reward. A big one."

He smiled. His eyes darkened. "I know, you mentioned that before. Why don't we blow this show and—"

"And no doing." Katie and Dirk faced us, identical smirks on their faces. "You're not leaving until we've had a chance to mingle," Katie said.

I stifled a groan, but knew my expression was not a

happy one. I'd finally decided to sleep with Cam, and now I'd have to wait. Guess I'd screwed up by not taking a chance earlier. Payback from the universe could be hell.

"We need you to fill out the table," she insisted. God knows who we'll get stuck with if seats remain open. Mrs. Crankshaw could show up."

Katie and I shared a grimace while Dirk looked interested.

"I think I'd like to meet—"

Katie's look stopped his words. "Hush." She slapped her hand over Dirk's mouth, ensuring his silence. "Don't tempt the gods."

Remembering my own unanswered plea from earlier, I nodded agreement. Instinctively, I knew our cantankerous former elementary school teacher wouldn't be near the high school reunion at the country club tonight. I hadn't even seen our high school instructors, but Fate has no apparent rules. Witness the earlier interaction with Nicole.

Ginger and her husband, Rob Howe, who looked the worse for wear but better than he had lately, joined us. He'd lost some of the flab he carried around earlier this year, but he remained out of shape. Deep frown lines remained, though no new wrinkles were in evidence. The couple had been working through some issues, and given Rob's tight jaw, it appeared they hadn't yet achieved total reconciliation.

We moved as a group toward the bar and armed ourselves for the pre-dinner meet and greet. Ginger had reserved a table near the door for us and we sat with our drinks. I knew I sure didn't want to risk standing in a crowd while wearing one of Ginger's dresses. Besides that, the matching stilettos were not my normal footwear. Guess I'd have to hang on Cam's arm in case I tripped.

Former classmates and their spouses/dates continued filling the dimly lit room. I glanced over the space, not having seen the country club before. The soft lighting did its job, lending ambience within the large rectangle-shaped ballroom. A requisite line of crystal chandeliers marched across the ceiling, leading to a wall of floor-to-ceiling windows overlooking the golf course. A late foursome straggled toward the locker rooms, the only occupants of the trim, green expanse as night fell.

Cam sat in the upholstered chair to my right, while Katie and Dirk settled on the left. Rob and Ginger were across from me, leaving just the two chairs alongside Rob and Cam open. Our table sported a small bouquet of mums in the school colors of white and dyed baby blue. Coordinated ribbons streamed from the vase onto the linen table covering.

"Wow, don't we all look pretty," Katie said. She looked at Dirk, but I chose to believe she included the rest of us.

"You look fabulous, Katie." And she did. Her curly black hair had been drawn back and up, leaving a few teasing tendrils at her forehead. She wore a figure-hugging strapless red dress that highlighted her curves. Dirk whispered in her ear. Her brown eyes widened.

Feeling as if I intruded on a private moment, I turned to Ginger. "Sweetie, you are gorgeous." Ginger also wore a little black dress but hers looked classic where Nicole's didn't. Of course, the understated diamonds at her neck, ears and wrists didn't hurt the overall effect. She had wound her red hair into a smooth French twist. Nicole Kidman never looked so good.

We had such a convivial table, I hoped the two remaining chairs remained unfilled. Turned out that the reunion gods weren't done messing with me.

Travis strolled up, followed closely by Nicole. "Mind if we join you?" Travis pulled out a chair and sat beside Cam without waiting for an answer, leaving Nicole standing.

Rob jumped and extended the remaining chair for her. She smiled at Rob, leaning against him before sitting. His gaze lingered on Nicole's pushed-up cleavage. He licked his lips. Nicole murmured and he bent closer, his arm along the back of her chair.

I wanted to reach across the table and slap Rob silly. Instead, I looked away, unsure how Ginger would take my interference in her marriage.

Ginger's mouth tightened, her cheeks reddened. Katie mouthed words at Ginger, who leaned back with a small smile. She sipped wine. When she replaced her glass, her hand hit the side of Rob's head. He sat back, blinking.

Katie winked at me. I knew I'd hear the whole story later. Good news travels fast.

Nicole leaned closer to Travis and captured his hand. Travis ignored her, instead studying Cam. "You look familiar, but I sure don't remember your name." He accompanied the statement with his trademark lop-sided grin. He pulled smoothly away from Nicole, extending his hand. "Travis Knowles."

"Cam Darrow. I graduated a few years behind you."

"Red Darrow's little brother? That's more than a few years, isn't it?" Travis's glance moved to me with eyebrows raised. His mouth had fallen open, but he clamped his lips shut and tried a debonair look. "So, you're what, from the class of 2004?"

Cam grinned at him and hugged my shoulders. "2006, but who's counting?"

I ducked my head and hid my smile. Dating a younger man had unrealized benefits, especially when confronting old, unfaithful boyfriends.

Cam must have put pressure into the handshake, because Travis's mouth had tightened into an almost grimace. Dirk, not slow on the up-take, gave Travis another strong grip when they were introduced.

Nicole, who abhorred losing the spotlight, jumped into the testosterone pool. "So, here we all are. Who'd have guessed how we'd turn out? Some of us successful, others not?" She studied the men. "And accompanied by such gorgeous males. I almost can't believe my luck."

As if the men had attended at her invitation. Without escorts.

Katie lobbed a lethal glare at Nicole and opened her mouth for a verbal blast when a cell phone sounded. Dirk grasped Katie's arm with one hand while the other reached for his inside pocket. Meanwhile, Nicole pulled a ringing phone from her purse. Looked like she'd been saved. For now.

She answered, "Daddy? What's wrong?"

Though she smiled, I noted what looked like fear race across her face. The mayor had raised Nicole as a single dad after her mother died when she'd been three. He'd marched Nicole across more speaker platforms than I cared to contemplate, and didn't look to be less demanding on her time now.

She rose, placing her hand across the phone's speaker. "Excuse me. I have some business. See you in a minute." Smiling at Cam, she sashayed off.

I heard her distraught reply. "But I did what you asked. I've worked hard when you needed me. Wait. Why should you get half—" She moved out of eavesdropping distance.

Maybe life as the mayor's daughter hadn't been so hot, after all.

Travis picked up the conversation. "So, Cam, what's your business?"

Katie leaned forward. "Cam works with me, Travis. At Get Solid Builders." She smiled at Cam. "He's a sweetie and our best crew supervisor."

Dirk settled back in his chair, his lips quirked up. He extended his arm across the back of Katie's chair. He looked like he'd enjoy some popcorn with the show.

A startled glance zipped across Travis's face. "Really." He addressed me. "You always did prefer jocks."

Katie's forehead crinkled. "What does that have to do with anything? Cam treats women like queens. He's no sleaze."

I shifted, uncomfortable, not relaxing even when Cam took my hand under the table. We'd waded into bad history, and even though people relive the past at reunions, I prefer the present.

"Travis, I hear you have your own company." Ginger to the rescue. "Want to fill us in?"

Travis's face lost its red hue as he described his investment firm. He and Rob had plenty in common, and they soon left the rest of us lost in industry speak.

Nicole returned along with the first course serving. Whatever her business had been, it hadn't been successful given her frown. She visibly shook off her funk and charmed Rob and Travis over gazpacho.

Only Cam's company helped me relax enough so I could choke down the meal. Nicole's presence at the table made no sense. Not until she addressed Dirk and made her strategy clear.

"Dirk, have you made any progress on Clarice's murder?"

So that's why she bullied her way into our group.

He glanced at her from under his lashes, his face expressionless. Putting down his drink, he straightened. "You know I can't comment on an open case."

She laughed, her trills grating in my ear. Once again, my last image of Clarice alive and resembling Nicole tickled my memory, as it had done several times over the past two days. I knew I should speak with Dirk, but now was not the time. And, the mistaken identity idea seemed kind of silly. Nicole acted like an ass most of the time, but that didn't mean someone wanted to murder her.

"Oh, come on, Dirk. Give us a break. We're all friends here. Besides, it'd be nice to announce that you've found the killer this weekend. Clarice was part of our class." She fixed her gaze on me. "You must have leads, right?"

Clarice's murder dominated the gossip rounds tonight, so Nicole's request for information could be considered reasonable. Except we all knew her question had an ulterior motive or three. Like asking for information when the investigator, along with the person who'd found the body, sat at the same table. She could simultaneously embarrass me in front of my friends and push for my arrest. I was glad Katie had broken the boy-girl-boy seating rule and sat next to me.

Dirk lowered his head. Running his finger through the condensation on his glass, he seemed deep in thought. Meanwhile, Katie glared at Nicole.

"Sorry. No comment."

"Well, have you at least figured out a motive for her death?"

Dirk shook his head. "Can't say."

"You'd answer if my daddy asked."

Dirk sipped his drink. "Pulling rank, Ms. Polk? I didn't expect *a friend* would put me on the spot during a social event."

I checked for steam over Nicole's head. No explosions yet, but her stare made an industrial-strength laser look blunt.

He sighed and pushed his glass aside. "Look Ms. Polk, I can't give you any answers. I pass information to my boss, and he talks with the higher-ups. That's the way it works. You want details? Ask my boss. Or better yet, your father."

Dirk stood and held his hand to Katie. "Come on, let's get a drink." They left the table and an ominous silence fell.

Travis threw back a shot, one of several he'd downed after joining us. "That went well, hey Nic?" He put his arm around her shoulders. "You used to be better at seduction."

She pulled away from him. "You're such an ass. I don't know what I ever saw in you."

Ginger, whose composure had grown progressively

cooler the more Rob flirted with Nicole, answered her. "Maggie. You went after Travis to hurt Maggie. That's what you saw in him." She took a quick sip of her drink.

Temper past control, I picked up the gauntlet Ginger had dropped. "I'm surprised no one has hurt you yet, the way you cat around. We've all heard the stories about you bopping Clarice's husband. You were in the spa at the same time. Could be you're the one who broke her neck. I hear Clarice's husband is loaded. Isn't that one of your criteria?"

"Me? I'm not the one with strong hands and arm muscles like a guy. She got killed on your massage table. I don't know why the cops didn't toss you in jail the first night."

I took a deep breath, ready to hit back. Good thing Dirk had left the table because I seethed, about to blow.

"Maggie couldn't hurt anyone," Ginger said. "She's a healer." Ginger's color had risen and her chin jutted out. "Not like some people at this table, who are better described as tramps."

Katie and Dirk hustled toward us. Silence had fallen in our part of the hall, as everyone at neighboring tables stopped their conversations and turned in our direction. Travis appeared almost sober, grabbing for water instead of a shot glass.

I caught Nicole's eye. "Clarice and I were friendly. I'd never hurt or use her." I heard my voice quiver and inhaled deeply. "Not for a man, not for money or status, never." Cam squeezed my shaking hand under the table and put his arm around my shoulders. "You are a nasty-ass back stabber. Why couldn't you have died instead of Clarice?"

Oh, shoot. When had I turned into one of the mean girls? I knew my conscience would eat at me for days because my temper had triumphed. I matched and held Nicole's angry gaze.

She threw her napkin on the table and stood, her chair legs squealing. "You're a bunch of losers. I've had it with this hick town. As soon as my investments pay off, I'm leaving. I don't need your crap."

Travis raised his head. "Bye, bye, Nic. Better make sure those 'vestments don't bite you in the butt."

"You should know, you loser," she bit off. She pushed a blowsy former drill team member aside as she stalked off.

The silence at adjoining tables rapidly segued into a low conversational buzz. Nicole's argument with my friends and me would hit the far sides of the ballroom in about thirty seconds.

I swallowed against the tension that filled my throat. Once again, I wished the past could stay unmolested. Perhaps other people had fond memories of high school. Not me.

Cam whispered in my ear. "Now I understand why you didn't want to come tonight. Let's get out of here."

I glanced at Ginger and saw that she and Rob were in a heated but low-voiced argument. Katie and Dirk stood aside, having their own intense discussion. My friends had stood by me. I couldn't walk out on them.

"Can't right now," I whispered back.

Cam took in the drunken Travis, fighting friends and empty seat at the table. He moved closer, putting his arm over my shoulder. "Then let's neck."

Yep. It coulda been senior prom again. I'll repeat: the untouched past is best.

Chapter Five

Cam and I didn't neck at the table, possibly the only thing that could have saved the dinner experience.

Nicole's empty chair acted as a portal, a siphon, or maybe a magnet, attracting people I didn't want to see. Or maybe the scene we'd caused earlier continually drew obnoxious people our way. After a series of embarrassing encounters, the next arrival had me in double-take mode.

His nametag read Bradley Crosby. Alias Sad Brad, class nerd and proven hacker extraordinary. This man must have arrived from another planet because he looked like no one I remembered.

Sad Brad had morphed into Bad Brad. As in bad-to-the-bone gorgeous. His once stringy blond hair curled over his nape in loving curls and waves. Broad shoulders filled out a suit that looked like silk to my tee shirt and denim jean accustomed eyes. His clothes caressed his frame in a huge change from the over-large, mismatched plaids he'd favored in school. He no longer walked hunched over as if protecting himself from the class bullies. Narrow frames replaced the dark, heavy glasses that had echoed Buddy Holly without the cool factor. Above and beyond the physical, Brad radiated confidence.

Brad's hand touched my shoulder, his fingers lightly caressing. "Hi, Maggie. Mind if I join you?"

He sat without waiting for my answer. In Cam's chair, not realizing my guy had gone for drinks. Oh, glory be.

No one had followed Sad Brad's progress after graduation. His mother had bragged to her friends who repeated stories, but I never paid much attention. On top of his unfortunate appearance, Brad had also been a Mama's Boy. That boy had disappeared, and given the looks from women at surrounding tables, was not lamented. Talk about your Clark Kent makeovers.

"So, Brad, how are you?" I gave myself high marks for biting back the question I really wanted to ask— what the hell happened? And, how long did it take you to grow from geek to glorious?

He moved his chair closer. "You look fabulous."

Travis lifted his head from contemplating an empty shot glass. "You." He hiccupped. "Still got the hots for Maggie, huh?"

Actually, it took me a minute to translate what sounded more like "hosh fer Meg-gurgle." When I did, I shot a glare at Travis, not that it'd hit him until tomorrow. If then.

I put my hand on Brad's arm, drawing his attention. "Ignore him. He's an ass." Throwing another barbed stare Travis's way, I turned back with a smile. "I'm surprised you're here."

Actually, no one I knew had bothered asking about Brad. We'd assumed he hadn't changed, and shame on us. No matter how nerdy, he'd gone through the torture of Granville Falls High School with the rest of us. Especially given the hell he'd suffered from the bigger, less intelligent guys in our class. And girls like Nicole. I wished I'd seen her face when Brad walked in. Talk about revenge. Yowsa.

Appearance pointed to Brad coming out a winner in the battle for most successful graduate if it had been put to popular vote tonight. Too bad Nicole had won that award this year. Knowing her, the honor had been her idea. I couldn't remember other classes bestowing recognition on one person.

Brad sipped from his glass filled with a brown-hued liquid. I had a feeling he didn't drink ice tea. He rubbed my shoulder with his as he shook hands and exchanged greetings with Rob.

"Why don't you sit at our table for a few minutes, Brad? If you can ignore Travis, that is."

Cam's warm hand squeezed my shoulder.

"Looking cozy, Maggie. Mind introducing me?"

I covered Cam's hand with mine. Making the introductions, I clearly indicated Cam as my date, but Brad didn't move. I waggled my eyebrows at Cam, and he took the hint and Nicole's abandoned chair.

If a headache didn't threaten, I'd have laughed. An old boyfriend, new lover and unrequited crush lined up beside me. I hoped Katie would continue hanging out on the dance floor. I could hear her comments now.

Dang. The comments were real, whispered in my ear. "Got your mojo working, huh?"

She plopped down next to me and made a point of reading Brad's nametag. "Brad?" She coughed. "Long time no see." Seemed she hadn't recognized Brad, either.

"Hi, Katie."

Cripes. He ogled Katie's neckline. Good thing Dirk didn't notice or his elevated male hormone level would choke everyone in the room.

Cam stood and moved behind me. "Mags, we haven't danced yet tonight. The next song is our special number."

After only six weeks of dating and no sex, not until we blew this place, we didn't have an "our song." I smiled over my shoulder at him. Either he wanted me away from Brad, or he'd moved to get us out the door. Either way worked for me. Brad's new look had made me uncomfortable. The changes in him were incomprehensible.

I stood ready to walk from the table when all hell broke loose. My foot connected with Brad's chair leg and when I jerked, I lost my balance and fell against Brad's broad chest. Meanwhile, Brad's flailing arms sent me flying toward Travis. My chair hit Cam in the stomach.

I'm not sure what all else happened, but the farce ended with me flashing Brad way too much cleavage, Brad falling toward Cam and several drinks soaking my boyfriend's dark shirt and silk tie.

Dirk had pulled Katie out of the fracas while Ginger and Rob looked on, mouths open. Katie covered her mouth and, I suspected, a huge grin. Dirk grabbed napkins and pushed them at Cam then helped me from Travis's lap.

Okie dokie then. Guess we didn't need much more of an excuse for leaving.

****

"He's harmless." I unlocked my front door and flipped on a light.

"I don't think so."

If Cam had sputtered after his pronouncement, I wouldn't have been surprised. "So tell me why you don't think he's harmless. Other than that he ruined your great tie." And shirt. And jacket. Likely his slacks too. I didn't want to check his shoes. If Cam and I hadn't been drinking vodka tonics, I knew he'd smell like a dive besides being partially soaked.

"This is a vintage Jerry Garcia design. Silk. My dad's from the 1990's. I only wear it for special occasions."

Dang. I knew I'd be heating up Amazon and my credit card looking for a replacement tomorrow morning. Or rather, later today.

Wait. He'd said "special occasions." My heart warmed. "Maybe Brad isn't totally harmless, but I don't think you can blame him for an accident."

Cam pulled off his jacket and plucked his shirt away from his chest. He lifted his tie, his fingers headed for the knot. "Ha. That was no accident."

"Let me untie that for you." I put my fingers on the knot and winced. This would not be an easy maneuver. "So besides your clothes, why do you think Brad didn't retain some clumsy dweeb genes?"

"I think he tripped you to set off the chain of events. Don't let his innocent act fool you."

One part of the knot loosened. Phew. Looked more likely I'd get him out of it before dawn. "Brad's I.Q. topped the charts but he never had social skills in school." I refrained from mentioning that the rest of him had caught up.

"He's got some muscle under those clothes. I'll bet he's coordinated, not clumsy."

I bit my lower lip. This second knot had no observable opening to loosen. "So Brad puts in gym time. I don't see why that makes him dangerous."

Cam pulled my hands away from his neck. His tie hit his chest with a splat. "Because, Mags, he's dangerous to you."

My forehead wrinkled. "Me?"

"Yeah, if any more drool had collected, you'd have been sitting in the deep end of a swimming pool."

Ah. The truth became evident.

"Katie starred on the swim team, not Brad. He golfed. Made varsity against all odds and held his own. That didn't change his status, though."

Cam grasped my upper arms, holding me—and Ginger's dress—away from his damp chest but still close enough to see his narrow pupils. "You know what I mean. I'm surprised your dress isn't soaked from his saliva." He ran his finger over the tops of my breasts.

I gripped his shoulders. "Is that the real reason you don't like Brad?"

He smoothed a fingertip over my cheekbones. "I didn't like the way he moved in on you."

"Your jealousy is sweet but unfounded. It's hard to see Brad in this new light. Kind of like the world tilted on its axis or something."

"From what I saw and heard tonight, Brad is out to prove he's no geek. Sheesh, your entire class held more than its share of liars, jerks and losers. And those are just the people I met." He pulled me closer. "Except you, Ginger, and Katie. You're rock stars."

What? I stiffened. The gossip lines must have been running hot and wide open. "What did you hear?"

"All good. Let's drop the subject. I've got something better to talk about." Cam kissed my forehead and nibbled his way to my lips and lower. "Help me out of these wet clothes?"

Oh, yeah. With renewed determination, that tie knot fell apart in no time. Our clothes disappeared and oh, my, seeing Cam nude? Better than I anticipated.

Shoulders from here to there, nipped waistline, muscle-packed thighs, and trim calves. My gaze moved to his penis and he acknowledged my stare by going from half to three-quarter mast in a nano-second.

Whew. Talk about delayed gratification. I hoped I returned the favor.

Apparently I passed muster and then some. His pupils expanded, his breath hitched. His gaze traveled from my head to toe and back. "Maggie, you're lucky I haven't seen you nude before tonight." He let out a breath. "No way I'd have waited this long."

"Wow. You sure know how to compliment a girl."

We moved together, his body solid against mine. The musky undertone I always associated with Cam became more pronounced. His planted kisses on my temples, cheekbones and jaw.

I ran my hands over him, not feeling a place that wasn't hard with either toned muscle or desire. "Wouldn't you like to lay down?"

He lifted and carried me to my queen-sized bed. We rolled to the middle. The mattress had always seemed big enough until I shared it with Cam. His broad shoulders spanned almost half the bed, not that I complained.

His palms framed my face. "You're sure about this?"

I nodded and initiated a kiss so hot he couldn't question my attraction.

He pulled back. "Because I don't want our first time to be the result of some old boyfriend shining around."

Apparently my kiss hadn't been so hot after all. I lounged over his chest, the better for eye contact in my dimly lit bedroom. "You've changed your mind?" I swallowed a lump of emotion. To bed or not to bed a guy. Screwed me up every time.

His thumbs massaged my earlobes, causing a shiver along my nape.

"No, I haven't changed my mind. I know you're the woman I want for keeps. It's just—"

"It's just that Travis and Brad's attention toward me made you think I'm using you. Because we haven't had sex yet, and tonight I changed my mind. As if they made me horny, and you're here to scratch my itch." I rolled off him. "Like you're only good for one thing." *Just like the bitch that screwed you over.* I hadn't voiced my last thought, but our mutual knowledge of his former fiancé filled the room.

"No, you're not like her." He lifted me and meshed our upper bodies, his arms holding me in place. Unasked questions filled his gaze.

I gave him the only answers I had. "I trust you. I want you for you."

His muscles relaxed under me. "I'm glad." He pulled my face down for a kiss.

Hot turned scorching. It didn't take long before moans echoed off the walls. Being a modest sort, I won't say more, except that adage about waiting for good things had become my new motto.

I don't know why I'd worried. Given the way he worshipped my body, Cam wouldn't leave me anytime soon. Especially given my whispered plans, detailing how I'd reward him for waiting on me so patiently.

Chapter Six

"You mean you didn't get a stomach-full last night?" I blinked at Katie and Ginger, who stood at my door, disgustingly bright and chipper.

"Nope. Get moving. We've got the reunion breakfast this morning." Katie grinned. "Besides, you owe us. We waited until Cam left before knocking." She slipped past me.

"I'm surprised Cam's tongue didn't get stepped on, what with it hanging on the floor every time he looked at you last night. Told ya." Ginger hugged me then joined Katie in smart-aleck grins.

Holding back a full-fledged smile proved hard, but I managed the task. "Thanks for lending me the outfit." I thought I'd hung up the garment, but couldn't remember. Things had gotten heated pretty fast last night, and I'd only rolled out of bed ten minutes earlier. Anyway, I'd planned to dry-clean the outfit and Cam's tie. A replacement J. Garcia had been found and ordered while Cam showered, but I still wanted the one his dad had given him as spotless as possible.

Katie leaned against the door. "Is the dress still in one piece, or did he tear it off you when you got home?" She cleared her throat. "By the way, did he rock your world? That man has some muscles. You did finally do the deed didn't you?"

Ginger nudged her.

"What? She looked hot-to-trot last night. And she's got beard burn on her chest this morning. Wait, is that a hickey?"

I glanced down and quickly pulled my robe tight. My face burned. "I, uh, we, um, we necked. Guess we got carried away." I continued my feint with little hope of success. "You know, like high school." I'd never felt comfortable talking about my sexual exploits, not that I'd had that many. But these were my closest friends. I shrugged and grinned. "No details, but yeah. Officially rocked my world."

Ginger grabbed Katie's shoulder. "Maggie doesn't want to talk about it. Geez. Maybe we should ask for a blow-by-blow about you and Dirk."

Katie plunked her hand on her hip. "I don't think so." She grinned at me. "The facts would send this place up in a fire so hot there wouldn't be any smoke. Just burnt out cinders too tired to wisp." She whispered into my ear. "Never mind, I get it. Cam's too new."

"Come on in while I grab a shower. Coffee should be done by now." When I walked into the kitchen fresh and dressed, my friends were munching Ginger's home baked cookies and lounging at the table.

I poured a coffee and checked the fridge for creamer. Shutting the appliance's door, I picked up the ongoing conversation.

"And then the fashion luncheon, unless you prefer golf," Ginger said.

Ginger had been on the girl's golf team, so I knew where she'd be heading. Katie hated exercise and fashion anything, so if I went to breakfast with them, I'd be off the hook until later today. Sounded like a plan I could support.

I'd barely settled at the kitchen table when Katie opened a new topic. "So, can you believe the changes in Brad Crosby?"

"He really grew into himself," Ginger said.

"With a vengeance." I taste-tested a cookie.

"Vengeance is right." Katie pointed to Ginger with a half-eaten cookie in her hand. "He didn't hold back about sharing his successes."

"Not everyone has a chip on their shoulder." Ginger huffed. "So he had something to prove. That incentive drives any number of successful people."

"Yeah, and he didn't look like a men's fitness magazine cover model in high school." I recalled my hand hitting his shoulder in the fracas after dinner last night. Cam had been right about Brad having muscles. Not that I'd mentioned my observations.

Katie leveled her partially eaten cookie in my direction. "I see you salivating over there. You'd better not even consider dumping Cam for that weasel Brad."

"I wasn't thinking about Brad in that way." Had I? My thoughts moved to last night's activities. Nope. Cam wouldn't get traded in anytime soon, if ever.

"Uh huh. I see where your thoughts went." Katie nudged my arm. "Go on, finish your coffee and get your purse. Hurry up."

I stared at her, wondering what had her all wound up.

"What. Nicole left by herself last night. I want to brag about hot sex with Dirk in front of her. You know, just loud enough for her to hear and get jealous. "

Eye roll action wouldn't have been out of place, but I restrained my urge. I'd reconciled myself to another day of forced enjoyment. After the dry cleaner stop, of course.

"Let's travel together." Ginger held up her keys. "I'll drive."

We tumbled into her luxury car and took off. I ran a hand over the soft leather upholstery, glad I'd left my coffee mug at home. Ginger wouldn't mind stains; I would.

Katie half-turned in the front seat. "Dirk's not talking about the case, the rat."

"What about Matt?" I asked.

Ginger answered. "Him either."

Katie picked up the complaint string. "I know they're looking into Clarice's recent relationships, financials, all that regular stuff. I couldn't get anything more out of him. And I tried."

Shifting on my seat, I leaned forward. "I can't help thinking Clarice's murder could have been a mistake. I mean, Nicole was in a different room, but she was supposed to be in mine. Liz offered her space to me, and I jumped on it. Otherwise, Clarice would have been in the reception area not in my room when the killer walked in."

"So you think the murderer meant Nicole as the target and missed?" Katie nodded. "Now that I believe. Nicole's someone who inspires murder."

Ginger slowed the car and glanced to Katie. "You don't mean that."

Katie looked out the side window then back at Ginger. "Guess not. She ticked me off last night, that's all."

Ginger shook her head. "She just acted like herself."

"Yeah, that's what I mean."

Someone who didn't know Katie would think her heartless, but I knew her loyalty had no bounds. Nicole had earned a place on Katie's shit list and wouldn't fall off anytime soon.

Ginger stepped on the gas, and we turned to other subjects. Still, I couldn't stop thinking I should call Dirk and share my crazy idea that Clarice had been killed by mistake.

****

Breakfast seemed more relaxed than I'd anticipated. A muted noise level, probably the result of hung-over participants, made the atmosphere enjoyable. My two friends and I snagged seats at an empty table set for four. Reserving our seats with sweaters and handbags, we made for the buffet line and began filling plates with fresh fruit and yogurt. I planned on returning for some tasty looking cheese grits, sausage, and fluffy eggs. Once you're raised on good old fashion Southern breakfasts, it's difficult to change. The cheese grits were enough of a departure from tradition, much less eating only fruit and yogurt.

Katie eyed my plate after my second buffet trip. "Girl, I don't know how you can eat like a truck driver and stay skinny."

I grinned, my mouth too full of delicious food for words. Not that she required an answer.

Once I'd swallowed, I leaned closer. "You'll wish you'd gone back for more when I tell you what I heard."

I looked around to ensure no one sat close enough for eavesdropping.

"You know where the fresh fruit bar intersects the hallway?"

Our three heads turned in unison. Yep. The inanimate bar remained situated right where I'd said. The station stood empty, a lucky coincidence or we'd have one confused person wondering about our combined stares.

"As I moved along the buffet, I could hear arguing. When I got closer to the end, I realized the angry voice sounded like one person, not two. I figured, phone call."

My friends nodded. Katie gave me the hurry up signal with her right hand.

"So, okay, I recognized Nicole's voice."

"Let me guess," Katie said. "That's what took you so long coming back." She nudged Ginger. "I told you she wouldn't have a problem deciding between the sausage and bacon."

They looked at my plate, which held both meats.

"So I like protein. Anyway, I stalled so I could hear more." Plus Katie was right. I really couldn't pick one meat choice over another.

Ginger spoke while her lips remained still like a ventriloquist's, a skill I'd love to develop. "What did you hear?"

I scanned the area again. All clear. "Nicole said she wanted her payoff. Said she couldn't wait to blow this small-minded town."

My companions raised their eyebrows, encouraging me to continue. "Then she said she 'knew the truth about' something. I didn't catch that part."

"Well, don't keep us waiting." Katie had slid to the edge of her chair and teetered there. "Then what did what did you hear?"

"A few words about 'investments coming due.'" I

chewed bacon, satisfied I'd piqued their interest and wanting to milk it.

Katie narrowed her eyes at me. "You know more than you're saying."

I swallowed the bacon but not my cat-in-cream grin. "I heard her say Daddy."

Ginger put her hand over mine, staying my food-filled fork from reaching my mouth. "Do you mean she talked with her father or to someone else about him?"

"I don't know. I couldn't hear that part because she lowered her voice." Plus, my head had been partially under the sneeze guard. I'd been reaching for a spoonful of hash browns, not wanting anyone to realize I eavesdropped.

"Huh." Katie rubbed her forehead with one finger. "I wonder if any of this is connected to Clarice's death. Or could our glorious mayor be getting his hands dirty?"

I grinned, knowing she'd adopted that forehead rubbing gesture from Dirk and hadn't realized she'd picked up his habit.

Ginger shook her head, her lips turned down. "Katie, tying a phone conversation to Clarice's murder is really far-fetched. And investing isn't against the law for a public official." She cocked her head. "Unless it's a conflict of interest."

Katie snorted. "Do you really think that nothing underhanded is happening?"

"You're seeing a crime where there isn't proof of one."

I stepped in. "All I'm saying is that Miss Nicole is not the squeaky clean former prom queen she portrays."

"Perhaps she is, and it's our interpretation of a one-sided conversation that isn't on the ups. Or could be her daddy got her involved against her will." Ginger always took the high road. Darn it all, anyway.

I mulled my other overheard phone conversation from the night before. Whatever Nicole had hooked into made her a very unhappy person. I decided to mention Nicole's whining but didn't get the chance.

"Ginger, stop being a goody two-shoes. I vote she or her daddy is dirty. I retain the right to accuse them both." Katie lifted her arm in physical support of her statement. "Any other yea votes?"

My right hand held half a jam-covered biscuit, so I raised my left. Ginger hesitated then joined our indictment.

"Are you girls taking a pledge about something? Don't you think you're a little old for the Girl Scouts?"

Nicole stood at our table. She must have approached in Ninja mode. Good thing Katie hadn't spoken Nicole's name when she made her accusation.

Ginger made the fastest recovery. "Hi, Nicole."

I stuffed my face with biscuit and looked away. Katie drank her juice, also avoiding a greeting. If I were Nicole, I'd be surreptitiously checking my armpits just in case I physically offended. I envied her confidence in all situations, but she didn't have to lord it over us. Especially after our public blow out the night before.

"Mind if I join you for a few minutes, Ginger? I know you're big enough to let bygones lie and do the reunion committee a favor."

No discernable apology there.

Katie and I exchanged glances. I concentrated on chewing, and Katie sipped her coffee.

"One of our models backed out of the fashion

luncheon today. I'd love for you to fill in for her. You have the right height and weight for taking the model's place. And your posture is perfect. Would you help us out?"

Pardon me? Ginger had made clear last night that she stood with Katie and me. I couldn't figure Nicole's angle asking for help with the fashion walk. Except that she knew Ginger's popularity never flagged. Nicole had just made an obvious bid to recoup her reputation. And an obvious slap to me—Ginger and I were the same size.

We really needed to stop leaving open seats at our table. They only filled with asses.

"Sorry, Nicole, but I'm golfing in a few minutes."

See, that's what I mean. Ginger is a princess.

"Ginger, your grace and style are matchless. Besides, we need a model that understands the French couture we're showing today. We have the latest from Pierre's. Won't you reconsider?"

Ginger's jaw tightened. I could sense her inner dilemma. She didn't want to hurt my feelings or give up golf, but a primary passion also drove her. Ginger not only loved gorgeous dresses, she couldn't resist wearing one whenever she had the opportunity. The clothing called to her. I knew the dress she'd lent me had whispered a siren's sigh in my ear the whole time I wore the garment. I couldn't imagine Ginger happily refraining from taking this opportunity. Especially as she'd bitched about not being asked by the committee during the event planning stage.

I chose to help her make the right decision. "Ginger, you know Katie and I would love seeing you wearing the latest French fashions. You should help out."

She bit her lip, but I saw the flash of gratitude cross her face. "I guess I can help. My golf partners left a few minutes ago. I probably won't catch them before they tee off."

Nicole smiled and stood and without looking at Katie or myself, thanked Ginger and left.

Now that we had a personal fashion show connection, Katie and I would cheer, whistle and stomp for Ginger at the luncheon. Our actions would not only support our friend, they'd tick off Nicole. We couldn't go wrong.

Chapter Seven

I spent the rest of the morning on tax paperwork, inventory, and ordering supplies. My bank balance usually hovered on empty, but if everything went well, I'd make my bills again this month. Dolores had offered me breaks when I couldn't meet my rent on time after I started out. I didn't want to backtrack and hated being in her, or anyone's, debt.

Katie and I met at the country club, but this time outside a smaller private room than the one used for the dinner dance the previous night. Once again, Nicole sat behind the reception desk. I wondered if she comprised a one-woman reunion committee. Wouldn't surprise me.

"Ladies."

The sarcastic tone she used didn't escape Katie or myself. We chose to take the high road and ignored her snark, knowing we'd get revenge later.

Choosing a table furthest from Nicole, we sat with four former classmates who lived out-of-state. We caught up and cooed at baby photographs. None of the babies were ugly, a true relief to me and I knew, Katie. I couldn't honestly compliment the mother of a jug-eared kid with blotchy skin. A comment about being handsome like the baby's father often backfired. Besides, everyone in town knows I can't lie worth a damn.

The luncheon passed in a pleasant haze of white wine and chicken salad. After the waiters cleared the empty plates, we settled in for the fashion show. Which didn't start.

I saw an opportunity to hit the bathroom before the lines got too long and took it. As I searched for the bathroom, I skirted the cocktail lounge just off the foyer. Two men were seated at the bar holding what looked like an intense conversation. Not so odd, except their builds and coloring reminded me of Travis and Brad.

I took a step toward the bar but before I could move further, a woman behind me offered assistance. After receiving directions, I turned and stopped. The two men had gone. I figured the duo may not have been my old classmates, anyway.

The ladies' lounge encompassed its name—a place I could hang in for an hour or so. A large flower arrangement dominated the table just inside the door. Pink-hued marble tile covered the floor and the walls to chair rail height. Low lights with, surprise, a pink hue ensured the women who walked in would look their best. The marble countertops boasted small soaps and cloth hand towels, not paper towels in a dispenser. A separate area held individual vanities with stronger lights, make-up mirrors, and short, upholstered stools.

No one occupied the room, not even an attendant, though I could see from a cup of steaming coffee that someone had just stepped away. Criminy. Seemed a shame to use this room for anything other than lying on the fainting couch and reading romances while eating bon-bons. Yes, the space included an armless sofa. I wondered if anyone would notice if I moved in. Good thing I didn't know about this room last night. I'd have found a way to lure Cam in here and lock the doors.

Really. All this opulence made me feel sexy. Also, my dark strawberry-blonde, green-eyed self looked really good in pink.

I stepped behind one of the louvered doors, happy the fixtures were porcelain, not gold-plated. If this room had proven any more opulent, I might have had to search out another bathroom.

At the sink, I washed my hands and used a towel. I looked around, not sure of what to do with the damp material.

I considered tucking the Egyptian cotton into my handbag when I saw a short laundry hamper beside the attendant station. Still unsure, I pushed open the top and dropped my towel onto the small pile already resting there. Then I scanned the table and my insecurities hit.

Holy Waterford crystal tip bowl. That's why I hated upscale places. Should I leave a gratuity when the attendant hadn't been present? Did you tip just because you used a towel? I didn't know and my stomach churned.

Figuring I'd leave something, just in case she came back before I could exit, I pulled out my wallet. A five-dollar bill and some pennies were all I found. I'd have to stiff the woman.

When I turned to go, my handbag hit the coffee cup. I grabbed it before it tipped completely over, but not before java splattered my jacket and onto my slacks. Shoot. A quick scrub with a damp towel took care of the stains. I scooted out the door before I owed the unknown attendant a tip *and* a replacement coffee.

Sliding into my seat, I scanned the room, glad

everyone still chatted while event volunteers scurried back and forth. Some of the volunteers reminded me of former cheerleaders or drill team members, but I couldn't be sure. I hadn't moved in those circles, and the intervening years hadn't been kind to everyone attending.

Katie turned from the former classmate seated alongside her. "What took you so long?" She noticed my damp jacket. "Did you have a run-in with Nicole or did you take a quick dip in the pool?"

I shook my head. "Neither. Tip bowl."

Katie's forehead scrunched but before she could ask me another question, a microphone squealed. We jumped.

"If Nicole Polk is in the room, would she please report to the front?"

Katie and I craned our necks along with everyone else, but no Nicole stepped forward. Knowing her penchant for self-glorification, that seemed odd. We both shrugged and resumed our separate conversations.

Several minutes later, the same volunteer called for our attention. "We'd scheduled the fashion show first with dessert, coffee, and a selection of liqueurs afterward. Our announcer has stepped away, so to hold our time line we'll switch the agenda." She pointed at the well-built college-aged waiter standing nearby. "Bring on the sugar!"

Laughter swept the room. I nudged Katie and rubbed my hands together. The caterer's desserts were renowned in Granville Falls. Katie had held up the probability of Elvis Pie in her arguments for assuring my attendance. Peanut butter, butterscotch caramel sauce, and chocolate toffee bar pieces all in a graham cracker crust. Yum, yum. If I didn't get a slice of that pie, Katie would hear me roar.

My saliva had built up a good head of steam when screams sounded close by. Katie and I jumped to our feet, headed for the nearest door. Following raised voices, we ran down the hall, through a door held open by two white-faced waiters.

Katie slid to a stop in front of a third waiter. "What happened?"

He shrugged. "Don't know. Sounded like the screams could have come from the walk-in refrigerator."

She ran in the direction of his pointing finger, yelling over her shoulder. "Call 9-1-1 now."

Instinct had me following more slowly, afraid of what I'd see. Still, I kept Katie in sight and saw her halt in the doorway. The walk-in refrigerator's location around the corner from the kitchen hadn't prevented most of the catering staff from collecting in the hall. Their ashen faces told me I shouldn't approach, but I did anyway.

I gained Katie's side and felt her trembling. Her shivers weren't from cold. Mine weren't either once I got a look inside the room.

A metal serving cart had tipped over with at least three Elvis pies sprayed over the floor. That gastronomic loss hadn't caused the screams, however.

Nicole's body lay face down on the floor of the walk-in refrigerator. It looked as if her face lay immersed in an Elvis pie. That alone could have been a horrific sight if not eclipsed by the handle of a chef's knife sticking from her back.

Moving carefully, Katie approached Nicole and

touched a pulse point. She shook her head and backed away from the body.

When she reached my side, I pulled her into a loose hug. "You probably shouldn't have done that."

"You're right. It's not like CPR would help her." She looked at me, her eyes blinking fast. "I just couldn't let her lie there without doing...something to help." She shrugged helplessly.

Katie fumbled in her pocked, yanking out her phone. She hit a speed dial selection and within seconds had her party.

"Dirk, get over here right now."

Nothing in her clipped tone could be confused with a seduction.

"There's a dead body in the country club kitchen's walk-in refrigerator. Nicole Polk." She closed her eyes. "We're fine." In a softer voice she said, "I'm okay, but please hurry."

Katie flipped her phone shut. Her voice faltered then strengthened. "Everybody move away from the door. Now. This is a crime scene."

At her words, the wait and kitchen staff backed off. They muttered in low voices but didn't leave the hallway. We stood in the doorway, figuring we'd discourage anyone else from entering.

My gaze surveyed the lined-up metal serving carts hosting an assortment of tortes, éclairs, and cheesecake tartlets. Along with the pies, a clear glass bowl holding trifle lay on its side on the floor. Whipped cream splatters decorated the knife handle. I realized that meant the trifle had been tipped over after the murder, when the perpetrator fled. Seemed like a panic move, because the noise would have attracted attention. Then I realized someone had acted fast in killing Nicole then avoiding detection. I hoped a witness had noticed the escaping criminal.

When the first responders arrived, the servers flattened against the wall but showed no signs of leaving. A few pulled out phones and snapped pictures of the paramedics wheeling in a gurney sporting a squeaky wheel. I realized then that the murder of a mayor's daughter would cause a non-stop media onslaught.

Damn. Not again.

My penchant for sinful desserts would be taking a hiatus. Sugar ranked high in my coping mechanisms list. Now I knew I might never eat Elvis pie again. None of these developments left me happy.

Dirk strode directly to Katie, looking like he wanted to envelope her in a tight embrace but he held himself in check. Matt continued past with two patrol officers. I heard him issuing orders inside the walk-in refrigerator. Then Dirk touched Katie's hand and turned away to work.

Poor Katie. Another dead body. Unfortunately, I knew how she felt.

She joined me. "Looks like you were right about Nicole as the target."

Once the initial shock lessened, I'd had the same thought. "I knew I should have talked with Dirk, but figured the call could wait."

"Not your fault." Katie patted my shoulder. Her quick, soft touch meant more than a bucket full of words from anyone else. "I should have told Dirk what Fiona told us about Nicole's fidgeting at her last fitting. I didn't think it important. Now we know she must have had a reason for nerves. Who can tell what's important?"

More patrolmen came in, and circulated, ushering everyone present into the kitchen. Katie and I grabbed seats, knowing the wait could be a long one. I didn't watch the clock but was glad we'd usurped the chairs. My shaky knees and fast pulse guaranteed I couldn't have stood upright for long.

Later, the gurney holding a zipped up body bag squealed past the kitchen door. A cop carrying an evidence bag with the pie followed.

Nicole and Elvis had left the building.

Katie and I exchanged glances, a good thing. I couldn't have carried on a conversation. Seeing my long-time nemesis wheeled out left my mind blank, my emotions at a standstill.

That's why getting called in for my police interview was the last thing I wanted.

Too bad I hadn't a choice.

Chapter Eight

"Sit down, Maggie." Dirk motioned toward a chair in front of his borrowed desk. I advanced into the country club manager's office and took a seat. Dirk hadn't smiled, so neither did I.

"Sorry we're meeting again this way," I blurted. Cripes, what a stupid thing to say. Apologizing as if I'd committed the murder.

He nodded and leaned back but kept his notebook and pen in hand. "Just start with when you arrived here today."

Matt placed a bottle of cold water on the desk in front of me. Nodding thanks, I cracked it open and took a long drink before answering.

"Actually, I didn't want any part of this." I sipped my water, stalling for time. Dang, I just kept digging myself a bigger verbal hole. Now I needed to explain why I'd been at the luncheon after that thoughtless sentence opening. Otherwise, he may think my reasons for attending the event were murderous.

Telling Dirk about Nicole's request of Ginger, and Katie's and my plan for supporting our friend, had him nodding. Katie could have filled him in, though I didn't know when they'd spoken together when I hadn't been present. Could be he nodded to keep me talking.

He asked me a few questions, but I told the story without excessive interruption. When I arrived at the point where we found Nicole, my throat closed up. Dang. I hadn't liked Nicole for years. Maybe never. But death is final, and I'd seen hers.

"Take your time." Dirk motioned to Matt, who replaced my empty water bottle with a full one.

I swallowed my nerves and finished my recollection. He nodded again and studied his notes.

"Tell me more about your interactions with Ms. Polk."

"You mean in addition to what you've already heard?"

He nodded.

I sighed. "We were polar opposites who'd fallen into a pattern years ago. Neither of us cared enough to break the mold we'd built."

"Molded in what way?"

I thought he might understand better if I explained our history. Even though I'd moved on from high school stuff, my experiences there had influenced me.

"Nicole reigned as Miss Popularity. Prom Queen, head of the cheerleaders, the preferred date of quarterbacks and basketball centers. She ran with the in crowd."

"And?"

"And nothing. We hung with different groups."

"So tell me about Travis Knowles."

My heart thumped hard and my stomach muscles twisted. Good thing I hadn't eaten much. "Travis?" My voice sounded helium tinged again. "We dated. Again, you could have figured that out at last night's dinner."

Dirk's fingers tapped a slow rhythm. "Why didn't you tell me earlier?"

"Didn't think it mattered. Clarice hadn't been

friends with either of us."

I swallowed my old sense of betrayal, wondering why memories still affected me when I'd been sure I'd resolved these issues. "In senior year, Travis won the Prom King election to Nicole's Queen. They hooked up for the dance. Not a big deal."

The detective's expression told me he knew the history. "Maggie, small town gossip hangs around a long time. The story we heard differs."

I set my coffee cup down harder than I intended. "Okay, so I argued with Nicole. We came to terms later." Kind of. Her prom photos were all taken right profile to hide her blackened left eye, courtesy of me. Yes, I had a temper I'd since mastered. Well, mostly had under control.

Dirk sighed. "Look, we don't railroad citizens. Several people," he paused so I knew they had to be bigwigs, "called me with the story. We check out all leads."

I returned his sigh and doubled it. "Nicole seduced Travis. She made sure I saw it happen." The image of Nicole lounging naked in her family's hot tub while Travis sat close beside her had stayed in my memory banks. The bucket of cold water I'd emptied over her head had only made her gasp then laugh at me. Travis just watched, already turned to the dark side.

I'd never understood his traitorous behavior or her spiteful pursuit of any boy who looked my way. Instead, I'd stopped thinking about her actions years ago and simply stayed out of her way where possible.

Dirk cleared his throat. "Anything else?"

"Travis had been my prom date, but we broke up before the dance." And after I'd given Nicole that black eye for a remembrance. "Look, that stuff happened fifteen years ago. Our paths rarely crossed. She shocked me when she called for an appointment." I'd wanted to tell her no way. But I needed rent money and now I stood in deep poop.

"Have you seen Travis since he arrived in town?"

"You mean besides the dinner-dance?"

Dirk nodded.

"He stopped by my house the other night."

Travis began his banking career in Chicago before starting the investment business he'd bragged about last night. I'd stayed home and nursed my mother. Had he not made a point of visiting me, or my friends forcing me to the reunion activities, there'd have been no chance we'd cross paths.

"Did you know he planned on attending your high school reunion?"

"No, we hadn't talked in years. Besides, I wouldn't have seen him. I hadn't planned attending the reunion."

Dirk's fingers tapped again. "Is that because Nicole would receive the Most Successful Graduate Award?"

"No." *Yes.* "Most of the events are being held at the country club. I don't have the clothes, the money, or most important, the inclination to attend."

He gazed at me, apparently wondering if I'd held a fifteen-year-old grudge. I hadn't, lurking memories notwithstanding. "It must have been hard to nurse your mother, lose your full scholarship, and watch your boyfriend defect to a rival all within the space of a few years."

All hope of answering that question, even if I'd been forced, was moot. It's hard to talk when your throat is closed up with remembered sorrow and old tears. I sat quietly, fighting for composure.

Finally my throat muscles eased and I swallowed. "What does any of that have to do with some nut case killing Nicole?" The answer came without thought. My voice raised in volume and tone. "Motive? You think I murdered Nicole? Clarice, too, probably."

Dirk raised his hand palm up. "Maggie, someone raised your history with Nicole and I need answers."

He dropped his palm. "You were out of the room for longer than a minute and when you returned your clothes had wet spots. Did you really think no one in a room full of women would notice and report?"

My hands shook. I pulled them onto my lap, clasping them tightly.

He continued. "Look, Maggie. You've been present at two murders." He cleared his throat. "We can't check leads we don't have. If you know anything about Nicole, new or old, tell me now. Otherwise, for your own good I suggest you think about calling a lawyer."

The echo of his statement rattled me like a chain swing in a high wind. If I couldn't help myself I'd be giving cot massages in the North Carolina Correctional Institute for Women. Nicole's dad would ensure it.

****

I stumbled through my door and collapsed on my sofa. Dang. A few hours repeating gossip about Nicole to Dirk had left my throat dry and my head spinning. Not that I had much hope the rumors would save me. One big fact loomed like a hawk over a field full of rodents. I'd been in an unattended lady's lounge at the time of Nicole's murder. I gave thanks Dirk hadn't booked me, especially given my outburst at the reunion dinner.

Exhausted, I picked up the ringing phone before checking caller ID. "Hello."

"Maggie, are you okay? Did you call a lawyer? Should I come over?"

I felt my chest rise and fall with a breath I hadn't known I held. "Katie." I inhaled again just because I could. "Yes, I'm okay. I should call a lawyer, but believing Nicole is dead is hard enough much less anyone thinking I could have killed her. You don't need to come over."

"No one messes with my friend. I'll be there in five."

I hung up, and before I knew it, Katie crouched in front of me holding a glass of water. She pushed it at me. "Here, drink this."

The water coursed down my throat before I realized I'd grabbed the offering. "Thanks."

She perched on the sofa beside me. "What did Dirk ask you?" She huffed. "If he treated you bad, he'll find himself sleeping in the hot tub."

I spotted an out from discussing my police interview and took it. "You're living with Dirk? I thought you two were "taking your time," and not rushing your relationship."

Katie blushed. "Yeah, well, you know."

Now she looked uncomfortable and I had to tease her. "Um, no. I don't."

She coughed. "I'm ah, renovating my bathrooms. Yeah, and I'm staying with Dirk until I get in the new toilets. They're on back order."

"Uh huh. You decided to tear up both bathrooms at the same time." My gloomy outlook lifted as my sense of humor surfaced. "Really."

The doorbell rang followed quickly by Ginger's voice calling, "Hello." Ginger saved Katie once again. Giving her a look that told her loud and clear I knew she'd lucked out, I stood and hugged our friend as she entered the room. At least now I avoided repeating an ugly story.

Ginger set down an overstuffed bag and pulled out a thermos. "I brought tea."

Katie perked up. "And cookies?"

Ginger tsked then looked at me. "Bring a plate. I've got cookies." She put her hands on her hips while eyeing Katie. "Kitchen sink cookies."

Uh oh. Ginger only baked kitchen sink cookies for dealing with dire circumstances. Didn't take a physicist to grasp my friends thought I stood neck deep in muck.

I pulled out mugs and small plates. Arranging those on a tray, I found napkins and carried everything to the living room. Katie and Ginger stopped whispering when I entered.

Ginger helped arrange the food and drink. Once we were settled, she leaned forward. "Tell me everything. I sat in a back room waiting for the start signal. Just my luck I didn't see or hear anything until later."

Katie and I exchanged tacit looks. We never wanted sweet-natured Ginger seeing another dead body, especially one who'd been stabbed in the back.

Backstabbed. I hadn't considered it that way earlier, but that's what she'd been. Had the killer left an unconscious message, or had the method of death been deliberate? Perhaps the weapon choice had been more a matter of using what was handy. Having known Nicole, I'd vote for deliberate. Now I sounded like Katie.

Damn. I'd called Nicole a backstabber when I'd told her she should have died instead of Clarice. In front of witnesses. Damn again.

Ginger bit into a cookie and relaxed into the sofa. "So what happened? I've been hearing all kinds of stories."

We took turns bringing her up to speed. "Stabbed in the back. That's telling, isn't it?" I was happy she didn't mention my incriminating comment at dinner.

Katie nodded and swallowed the cookie she'd been chewing. "Yeah, and coupled with Maggie's idea that Clarice's murderer really targeted Nicole, looks like the slime bucket finally got his victim."

"Aren't you jumping to conclusions?" I asked. "Could have been a woman who murdered Nicole. She screwed around so much an angry wife makes more sense."

She paused with a cookie at her mouth and shook her head. "You didn't see the knife up close like I did. The hilt had been buried." She laid her cookie on a napkin. "Had to be a guy. I'm not sure a woman could have hit her with that kind of force."

I gulped. "Unless the woman is a massage therapist with strong arms and hands."

They turned big eyes my way. "I'm not saying I did it. Just that I'm not ruled out."

Katie leaned forward pointing a finger at me. "Don't say that. Don't even think you could be considered a suspect."

Ginger nodded her head. "Katie's right."

My head bounced once against the back of my chair. I closed my eyes. Maybe my friends believed I couldn't murder anyone, but did Dirk?

Chapter Nine

"You need a good lawyer." Ginger covered her mouth. "No, don't think that."

I opened my eyes. Once again, she read my distressed thoughts perfectly.

"We don't think you killed anyone, but you were present at two deaths, one of them the mayor's daughter."

"Yeah, and if he listened to Nicole even in passing, he knows the two of you were not best buds," Katie said. "Plus reports about the fight you had last night is all over town."

"Well then, I'd better hope the public defender is a hot shot. Because I sure don't have the money for anyone more upscale. I can't even—" I stopped before admitting I didn't know if I could make both my rent payments.

"Don't worry about it," Katie said.

"What Katie meant," Ginger paused and sent Katie a look, "is that we'll help."

"I don't think so."

"It's not a thinking matter," Katie said. She turned to Ginger. "What. Stop giving me those looks."

Ginger's sigh echoed in the room. "What we mean is that my father helped a young lawyer get started some years back. I'm pretty sure he'd listen to your story. No cost involved. As a favor."

I bit back my skepticism that the type of high-powered lawyer I needed would see me for free. The psychic price I'd face would not be cheap.

"I'll find some way to pay you back, Ginger."

Because we're friends, though not as close as she and Katie, Ginger didn't insult either of us by denying that she'd foot the bill.

"Let's talk about that later. So, you agree I can call Tom Jenkins?"

"Tom Jenkins? That name is familiar."

"Yeah, he's in the news a lot." Katie gestured with a cookie. "He's the criminal attorney that takes only high profile cases. You know, like the record producer who killed his partner last year."

"High profile" meant expensive. "Ginger, I can't let you do this."

"Oh yes, you can. What good is having connections if you can't help friends?"

"Besides," Katie chimed in, "we'll help investigate."

Ginger crossed her arms. "Katie, I'm not so sure you should cross Dirk. You know what he told you this morning."

She flipped her hand as if shooing a fly. "I never promised." Before Ginger could say more, Katie continued. "Besides, don't you think it's time our capes came out of storage?"

Capes? I puzzled that comment while the two friends exchanged long looks. The only capes I remembered them having were vinyl ones in grade school.

Ginger nodded. Katie whooped. "All right! The Demonic Duo rides again."

I rubbed my forehead. Dang. This development couldn't be good.

****

I climbed into the backseat of Katie's car late Sunday morning. Once again, they'd talked me into a reunion event, a charity basketball game. At least the game ended the reunion weekend. But that didn't explain my friends' strange appearance. What they wore didn't look like Pep Club uniforms.

"We've gotta get you a cape." Katie studied me in her rear view mirror. She glanced at Ginger. "That means a name change from the Demonic Duo. You know. Because there are three of us."

"Don't push Maggie if she doesn't want to join us. Not everyone is excited about running around in short vinyl capes carrying purple batwing-shaped flashlights and half-masks." Ginger smoothed a lock of hair over her ear.

Katie ran a hand over her wrinkled cape. "I don't see why she wouldn't jump at wearing this cool costume." She rubbed at a deep crease. "I should fold it better when I store it next time."

"Store it? You call tossing it into that mess in your hall closet storing it? Haven't you left it in your car's trunk for the last couple of months?" She leaned closer. "What's that stain?"

Ginger straightened her immaculate cape. "I feel like Felix from The Odd Couple of crime fighters sitting next to you."

Katie snorted. "Yeah, and you just happened to have your cape packed into your bag along with cookies. We're some kind of Demonic Duo."

Their good-natured bickering dissolved my

apprehension about attending the game. I couldn't help myself. I burst out laughing then sobered. "Demonic Duo? More like Devoted Duo." Shaking my head, I leaned forward and clasped each of their shoulders. "Thanks, but I won't butt in. You're a team." I tried stopping my laughter but couldn't. "Besides, there is no way in hell I'd be caught dead looking the way you two do right now."

Katie snorted. "No fashion sense. Our capes are collectibles. Vintage."

Ginger turned and patted my hand. "Don't worry. We're not wearing these outside of the car." She fingered the vinyl covering her arm. "The capes are our good luck charm, but we don't flash them in public. At least not in daylight."

I had a feeling the silliness was also my friend's way of lightening my mood. In that case, given what I faced, I knew I'd see their capes again.

Katie snapped her fingers. "Got it. We can call ourselves the Triple Threat Trio, T-Cube for short." She eyed me in her mirror. "Tell me you can pass up this opportunity for becoming a crime fighter, and I'll know you're lying."

I relaxed against the back seat, stomach muscles cramping with laughter. Once I caught my breath, I gave up the protest. "Okay, but I'll travel incognito. What's our next move?"

"I don't know about you, but I'm taking off my cape. It's too darn hot." Katie opened her door and slid from the front seat. A moment later, the cape landed in my lap, its edges fluttering for a moment like a live thing. "Just stuff it behind my seat," Katie said as she got back behind the wheel.

So much for careful storage. I folded her cherished bit of vintage vinyl before laying it on the seat beside me.

Ginger had removed her cape and formed it into a compact package. "What's next, T-Cube leader one?"

Katie paused with her hand on the ignition key. "We need an action plan, T-Cube leader two."

Caught up in the play but fully aware my innocence remained at stake, I posed a question. "We have to hit the dang basketball game, don't we, T-Cube leaders?"

Looking over her shoulder, Katie pursued her lips, her forehead wrinkled. "That we do, T-Cube leader three. That we do." She started the car and drove off.

We arrived at the high school campus and a parking lot rapidly filling with cars. As I'd noted before, violent death attracts ghouls, and we were haunting with the rest of them.

I'd been surprised this last reunion event would take place as scheduled. Ginger said she'd heard the mayor had insisted. I didn't want my mean girl side showing up again, but couldn't help wondering at the man's motives. Sure, the annual charity game had become a sellout due to the out-of-town reunion attendees, but wouldn't it make more sense to reschedule? My not-so-hidden mean girl smelled a political objective. Not surprising given what I knew of the mayor's use of Nicole as campaign platform "decoration."

The planned game opponents were our class's varsity team and the current one. Both teams had won their district championship, and I'd heard bets were laid all over town. The odds boiled down to youth and speed versus age and experience. Either way, given the turnout, the Granville Falls Fire and Rescue charity fund would win.

We entered the gymnasium. It hadn't changed much in fifteen years. A few more championship flags hung from the ceiling, and the bleachers looked new. I looked at the back wall. The scoreboards had also been replaced. Other than that, the recognizable odor of rubber, floor wax, and warm, sweaty bodies filled my nostrils. It almost made me nostalgic for high school.

The gasps and whispers began softly, followed by pointed looks and fingers extended in my direction. I sat between Katie and Ginger, my face red and not from the room's heat.

Ginger leaned into my side. "Ignore them."

Katie leaned into my other side. "Brainless A-holes."

"Katie," Ginger snapped, "Watch your language."

"What. What did I say? Besides, no one is sitting close by."

Her observation looked correct. We comprised a small island in the stands.

My friends' familiar interplay didn't help me relax. I wondered at the intelligence of attending the game when my reputation—my life—remained on the line. But consensus stated someone from the graduating class of 1999 lurked behind both murders. And today, most of our classmates would be right here. Including, we hoped, the villain.

Both teams were warming up, shooting hoops, and running the ball on each side's half-court. Then the mayor entered and all noise died. He approached center court, followed by a small contingent of political hacks and assistants.

He thumbed on a microphone, his throat clearing loud in the silence. "Good afternoon. As you know, my daughter Nicole was a driving force behind the class reunion this weekend. She had also won the Most Successful Graduate Award, which she would have received at the halftime ceremony.

"Nicole committed herself to many efforts, and I am proud of her accomplishments, especially given her life ended too soon. In Nicole's honor and remembrance, I asked that today's game be dedicated in her memory. I know that's what she would have wanted, and I appreciate the many cards and calls I received from my loyal constituents.

"Thank you for your concern and expressions of sympathy." He handed the microphone off but not before his last muttered remark of "let's get the hell out of here" transmitted to every ear in the place.

Through his speech, I sat stiff, not speaking to my friends. I looked straight ahead, but in my peripheral vision noticed people's necks craning my way. Their heads whipped around at the last comment. Had the mayor really said that and if so, had his words come from grief? Or had something besides emotion prompted the words?

Katie began speaking. "What the...oof."

Ginger had reached across me to grab Katie's arm. "Let's not talk about this now. We don't know who'd hear us."

I silently agreed. The seats around us had filled in, with one of the final spaces taken by Brad. He crammed in beside Katie.

"Hi, girls."

We chorused an answer and were prevented from speaking by the National Anthem, sung by Suzie Carter, another of our classmates and a Nashville wannabe. The tip-off followed, eliminating any need for conversation.

My gaze followed Travis moving around the court. He'd been an outstanding small forward in high school and had retained his youthful athleticism. It looked like he'd refrained from drinking too heavily the night before, or else he ran hangover free, because he jumped, passed, and blocked with the moves of old. At halftime the alums were down by four points. Not too shabby for the old guys.

Katie stood. "I'm going for a hot dog. Anybody want anything from the stand?" She took our orders and squeezed past Brad, who moved closer.

I decided to pump Brad for information, if only to satisfy my curiosity. "So Brad, I don't remember if you told us what you're doing now."

"I'm the CFO for BCI."

A proven hacker, Brad employed at a large computer software firm seemed almost cliché. His position as CFO still threw me a curve.

Ginger joined our conversation. "How'd you reach the executive office so quickly?"

Brad put his arm around me. "Hard work and lots of it." He threw me a wink. "Do you doubt my talents and ability?"

His raised eyebrows and curved lips left Ginger blushing.

Brad's arm slipped off my shoulder after I shrugged my answer.

Ginger straightened. "No, not at all. I guess after

you hacked into the World Bank, we all figured you for success. Just in a different way." She put her hand over her mouth. "I shouldn't have mentioned that old story. Sorry."

Brad nodded his head. "That's okay. Not a problem. I was a kid when it happened. You know. I got scared straight after that."

Ginger pursued her conversation. "I heard you attended MIT."

"Yeah, well, that didn't work out. I did a year at MIT, came back to state and got an MBA." He shrugged. "If I'd stayed in computers, I'd still be Sad Brad." He put an arm around me again and squeezed. "Instead, I'm seated with the two most gorgeous girls at the game."

I caught Ginger's eye. Brad only sat with us because he'd invited himself. The thought that he'd remembered his high school nickname made me wince, though. Seeing Brad's unguarded expression threw me. It's as if he read my mind, or at least suspected my thoughts. A flare of anger lit his eyes then dimmed.

"Well, we're glad you came back for the reunion," Ginger said.

"And I'm happy for your success," I added. "You've done yourself proud."

Brad's posture relaxed, but his expression became guarded again. That quick flash of anger could have been a reflection from the gym lights.

Katie's voice sounded. "Make way, come on, suck it up and let me pass. I've got a box full of food and drinks here. You don't want it in your lap if I trip."

Brad's muscular thigh pressed against mine. His body heat added to the already warm gymnasium temperature. If I hadn't hooked up with Cam, I'd certainly be intrigued with Brad's metamorphosis. His boasting made me uncomfortable, though.

Katie's arrival coincided with the teams' return for the second half. We settled in to cheer the "old guys" on to victory. Either the current team felt sorry for the grads or our team caught their wind and a winning strategy at half time. All I know is we screamed ourselves silly. When the alumni won by two points in a spirited flurry of shots in the last thirty seconds of the game, we felt vindicated and ready for alcoholic throat soothers.

Ginger, Katie, and I, followed by Brad, climbed down the bleachers and joined the teams milling on the floor. Travis surprised me by putting his arms around me from behind and pulling me against his sweaty chest. Good thing I hadn't worn a favorite outfit.

"Hey, Maggie," he whispered in my ear. "Remember how we always celebrated team wins?"

Before I could escape his embrace, he whirled me around and planted a big one right on my lips. I pushed away and saw Cam standing behind Travis. He did not look happy. Nope, his expression resembled dark and dirty.

"Cam, I'm glad you're here." I grabbed his arm, which stiffened underneath my hand. Dang. Looked like I had fast-talking excuses in my near future.

Then I saw Dirk and Matt enter the gym. If their steady progress toward me and deadpan expressions were an indication, I had more than one man in line wanting an explanation.

Chapter Ten

They stopped before me.

"Dirk. Matt."

"Maggie, we'd like to speak with you about some additional evidence." He ran one hand through his hair. "At the station."

Katie stepped forward. "Does she need a lawyer present?" He didn't answer. "Dirk? Does she?"

He answered through clenched jaws. "We just have a few questions, Maggie. Would you come with us?"

Cam's thunderous expression hadn't lightened, so in one sense I'd been saved by the cops. I nodded. "Sure. Should I follow you? I'd need to stop home and get my car, first."

Dirk hesitated and my pulse stuttered. "Why don't you come with us? We'll drop you at home later. You rode with Ginger and Katie, right?"

Shoot. Had they been tailing us? No, I'd just told him I didn't have my car. Geez, talk about paranoia. I nodded to him. "Okay."

Katie grabbed Dirk's arm and whispered into his ear. I saw him shake his head. He touched her cheek then his hand dropped. Wheeling, he joined Matt and me, and they escorted me toward the door.

We'd traveled no more than ten feet when Ginger called out. "Does Maggie need a lawyer present?"

Dirk turned to me and said, "You can request a

lawyer when we reach the station, or call on the way. We only have a few questions at this time."

"I don't have anything to hide, Dirk. I didn't kill anyone."

In my peripheral vision, I saw Ginger paw through her bag and pull out her phone. My stomach dropped. I knew she'd be calling her expensive lawyer friend for me. Ginger and Katie would never let me down, but I'd be giving Ginger free massages for my lifetime and still not finish paying her back.

Especially if my massage practice ended with a murder conviction.

The drive to the station didn't take long, in spite of the fact that none of us exchanged words. We wound our way toward Dirk and Matt's desks, settling at Dirk's. He yanked open a drawer and pulled out an evidence bag holding a sheet of paper.

"Does this look familiar?"

My hand shook as I grasped the bag and pulled it closer. I almost dropped the evidence when I saw a piece of "From the desk of Maggie Stewart" note pad paper inside. I switched my gaze to Dirk.

"Where did you find this?"

"Did you write that note?"

I'd been so shaken at seeing a familiar piece of paper inhabiting an evidence bag, I hadn't noticed the block printing underneath the heading. I read the message aloud.

"Meet me outside the walk-in refrigerator in five minutes." A blurred initial followed, one that could be interpreted as an "M," but just as easily another letter.

"What hallway, when, and where? I didn't write this. Or print it, either." I flipped the bag over but the back of the note was blank. "Where did you find this?"

Dirk and Matt exchanged glances.

"Come on, guys. You asked me here to answer questions. I can't answer them if you don't give me a clue what you want." I leaned against the chair back. "Look. It's been a long couple of days. At least give me a hint."

Dirk cleared his throat. "First, can you tell me where you store this note pad paper?"

"Sure. I've got a small desk in my massage room. I keep pads handy for giving my clients notes about water consumption, appointment changes, that kind of thing. You know."

"So multiple pads sit on top of your desk. Anyone has full access? Have you missed any of your supplies?"

"Yes to the first question and no to the second. What's this about?"

Dirk ran a finger around his collar. "Maggie, take a look at the note. Do you recognize the handwriting?"

"No, except that even though the handwriting is similar to mine, I didn't write this. And the creases indicate it had been folded in quarters. Where did you find it?"

"The Medical Examiner found it in Nicole's bra." Dirk leaned forward. "During their autopsy."

I felt the blood draining from my head. I couldn't move, even if my body hadn't shocked into paralysis by his words. My mouth opened and closed until I finally squeaked out, "Where?"

Dirk held my attention with a steady gaze.

After swallowing several times, I had regained enough saliva for words. "No. I repeat. I didn't write that note." My glance shifted between the two detectives watching me. "I wouldn't have met her secretly."

I thrust the evidence bag at Dirk. "It's not mine." My brain began working. "Are my fingerprints on that paper? No, wait, they can't be because I didn't write the note. Unless I touched the note pad, which is likely."

Dirk ran his fingers through his hair. "Maggie, are you sure no one saw you in the ladies' lounge during the luncheon?"

"I told you. No attendant showed." I snapped my fingers. "What about the coffee cup I grabbed so it wouldn't fall over? Remember? I know I told you about that. You found the cup, right? Wouldn't my fingerprints on the cup prove I'd been there?"

My thoughts galloped, moving along the path of proven innocence. They hit a roadblock when Dirk responded.

"The attendant said she saw no coffee cup at her station when she returned. She's not allowed to have drinks or snacks on duty, so it didn't belong to her." He ran his fingers through his hair. "The trash had been picked up, the waste basket empty."

"But you checked the cleaners, right? Maybe she remembered tossing the cup out."

He shook his head. "The woman on duty had a sick kid. She was on her phone and working by rote."

My heart stopped. That's the only explanation I had for no discernible pulse and zero thoughts. The roaring in my ears supplied the only clue I still lived. Unless strong winds accompany the light at the end of the tunnel.

Dragging my attention to Dirk, I thought I noted a

sympathetic glint in his eyes before his expression shuttered.

"I...I didn't...oh, god."

A strong voice called across the room. "Ms. Maggie Stewart?"

My head could have used a crane to accomplish the simple acts of lifting, turning, and nodding, but I got the job done without one. "Yes?"

The new arrival had light brown hair and a build that showed off his preppy weekend wear to perfection. He strode rapidly but with an economy of motion that hinted at expensive tennis lessons. Top-of-the-line running shoes covered his feet and a platinum faced watch glittered and reflected the fluorescent lights. This guy had money and spent it well.

"Don't say another word." He walked forward, his right hand extended. "Tom Jenkins." The blank look I knew decorated my face must have clued him that my mental abilities had shut down. "Your attorney."

He faced the detectives. "I want to see the evidence you have, starting with whatever is in that bag."

Matt handed him the note. Tom read the message without picking it up. He looked intently into my eyes. Whatever he saw in my expression—make that soul because that's where his stare delved—cemented his decision.

"I'll allow a handwriting sample. Oh, and I'll want a copy of whatever sample you take. I'll have my own expert make a comparison."

He looked back at me. "Don't say another word without checking with me first."

Turning to the detectives he said, "Next question?"

Dirk stood. "We've covered everything, except the

writing sample, for now. Maggie, we'll need you to copy off the words on this note." He tapped the evidence bag. "After that we'll give you a ride home."

Tom Jenkins helped me to my feet. "You've questioned my client long enough without representation. She'll come by tomorrow morning and submit a handwriting sample then."

Dirk stared at my attorney for a long moment. He stepped back from the table. "Then we're done here."

"Come on, Maggie. I'll take you home."

He led me to his imported luxury car and installed me in the front seat before climbing in on the driver's side and pressing the ignition. "Okay, what's your address?"

His question caught me off guard for a moment. I guess I'd thought my knight with a law degree knew everything already. Plus my thoughts were still hung up with the incriminating note I'd been shown. He punched my home address into his GPS, and we pulled away from the curb.

"Okay, here's how I operate." The GPS voice, a sultry female, interrupted with instructions to make a right turn in one mile. "If the cops stop you on the street, call me. If the cops telephone you at home or at work, call me. If the cops e-mail or social media you, call me. If the cops call you in for an interview—"

"I'll call you." I left off rubbing my temples. "Just one thing."

He gave me his attention.

"What's your number? I've never met you before."

"I'll give you a card with all my contact information as soon as we reach your house." He returned his gaze to the street, but I believed I still retained his attention.

"Sorry I can't meet with you tonight. I have a prior commitment." He flipped on a signal and made the turn. "I left one of my junior partners in charge of the grill and the guy can't flip burgers worth a damn." He smiled. "Great researcher, though."

We arrived at my residence. He reached into his console and pulled out a business card. After scribbling on the back, he handed me the cardboard rectangle.

"I added my unlisted home number. Don't give it out, but do call me if you need me after hours."

Taking his card, I hesitated with my other hand on the door handle. "I don't get it. Why did you come personally? You have a party underway. Wouldn't an assistant have gotten the job done for you?"

He tapped his index fingers on the steering wheel. "When anyone in Ginger's family calls, I answer." He leaned over and released my door. "Come in at eight o'clock tomorrow morning. I'll see you before my first court appearance."

I slid off the leather seat and stood in my driveway. Shutting the door with a solid click, I watched as my attorney's vehicle moved off with a quiet purr.

****

If I hadn't already heard that Tom Jenkins's reputation, and retainers, were top notch, I'd know it by his office. Well his reception area, which comprised the extent of all I'd seen so far.

He and his partner, Ed Fotherington, employed a woman for the front desk that I knew had done local modeling. I remembered her from a car dealer's billboard. She may also have graced the side of a bus for a while. Her photo, I mean.

Along with cover girl, cushy leather club chairs, an unlit gas log fireplace, and solid wood tables topped with designer lamps underscored the firm's importance. My first thought on entering had been that I'd ended up at the country club in error.

Cover girl offered me coffee, which put her on my list of favorite people. I'd no sooner finished doctoring it when she ushered me to the conference room and Tom Jenkins.

The attorney wore a beautifully tailored suit that reminded me of something I'd seen on the body of an actor attending the last Oscar ceremony. He looked rested and not much older than me, which put him in his mid-to-late-thirties. Briefly, I wondered how he'd settled in Granville Falls.

"Glad to see you, Maggie. Have a seat."

I doubted he expected a "happy to see you" reply, and he didn't get one. As I wondered what comment to make, a younger woman walked in and settled at the table alongside Tom and across from me.

"Maggie Stewart, meet my top assistant, Leah Mason."

They pulled legal pads and pens from a stack at the table's center. "Let's get started." He checked his watch. "I must leave for court in about an hour. If we aren't finished by then, Leah will complete this initial interview with you."

His first question gave an indication of how my next hour would go.

"Tell me why anyone would believe your innocence, considering the history you shared with Nicole Polk."

That's when I knew the uphill battle I faced had a

Matterhorn-like incline. I'd been worried before. Now I feared for my life.

****

I left Jenkins & Fotherington with a mushy brain and caffeine high. Then I stopped at the police station, where I left a handwriting sample without seeing Dirk or Matt.

Katie had design work due at Get Solid Builders, but Ginger waited for me outside GFPD headquarters. We exchanged hugs and agreed to relocate to Java the Hutt. Once settled with a pastry and a mug of decaf, I took my first full breath since rising.

"You know, Ginger, I'm wondering where Clarice's murder fits in this mess."

"Why?"

"I'm not sure. At first, I thought she'd been mistaken for Nicole, but now I'm questioning if that's right."

My friend tapped her fingers against the tabletop. "You've got something. I've heard Clarice had a pile of money in a personal bank account."

"Really? Huh. I mean, where did she get a bunch of cash? I didn't think she had a high level job, and her husband, well, what's his career field? I can't remember."

Ginger shrugged. "Don't know, but I heard it at the Hair Shack, so you know the info is probably true."

As the original hair salon in town until Charlotte spread our way, Hair Shack customers included the wives of Granville Fall's entrenched politicians and financial hierarchy. If the men knew what information their wives exchanged, the grapevine would wither in a New York street second. Or not. Many of the women were tougher than their husbands.

My conclusions jumped into words. "So her husband was afraid he'd lose the cash in a divorce. He could be the murderer. I need to tell Dirk."

Ginger held up her hand. "Already called Katie. She'll handle it. Besides, you should speak with Tom Jenkins, first. He'll talk with Dirk for you."

Chastised, I pushed a lock of hair behind my ear. I'd been responsible for myself for so long the thought of acting through a liaison remained foreign. I hoped I wouldn't screw up.

"How much money did her account hold? Did anyone say?"

"Not sure. Around a quarter million, according to someone who overheard Clarice arguing with her husband."

"What?" I ducked my head and lowered my voice, hoping the attention I'd caught with my exclamation would die down. Looking at her from under my lashes, I whispered, "Really?"

She nodded. "Apparently she ran a consulting firm." Ginger leaned closer. "But what's strange is that she didn't maintain an office."

Two other questions popped up. What kind of consulting paid that well, and if legal, how could I sign up? Before I inquired about either, Brad entered Java the Hutt.

Ginger and I gave little waves. She turned toward me with a small frown. "I wonder why Brad is still around. Yesterday the police told the out-of-town alumni they could leave."

"If I were them, I'd have left too. One more event could have meant one more murder."

Brad turned from the counter with a cup in his hand. He'd caught my eye before I could turn away and walked toward us. "I suspect we'll hear about it after he reaches our table." I pushed my face into a pleasant expression.

"Hey, Brad." Ginger smiled at the former dweeb turned doable. "You on your way back to California?"

"Nope, though I should leave soon. A back burner deal is heating up." He pulled out a chair and sat. "Mind if I join you?"

"Sure, Brad," I said. "Grab a chair." Ginger raised her eyebrows but Brad didn't catch the unintended sarcasm. Or if he did, he ignored my comment.

"Mom wanted me to spend this week with her. You know, because I don't get home often. I put in a lot of hours at work. Necessary, you know."

Ginger tilted her head. "I believe it. You and your fast track action." She shook a finger at him. "No time for the people you left behind."

I watched red wash into Brad's neck. For a moment he resembled the vulnerable Brad I remembered.

"You sound like my mom."

"So do you have a girlfriend?" God bless Ginger. She has more tenacity than a bulldog has teeth. But I couldn't figure out why she pursued this update.

He laughed, his capped teeth gleaming. "Now you really sound like my mom." His phone pealed. "Saved by the chime." Checking the number, his smile faded.

He held up his cell. "Company call. Nice talking with you. I've got to go." He hurried from the shop.

Ginger grinned. "I just had to know. Some things never change. Brad may be gorgeous now, but he's still a dweeb at heart."

I chewed my bottom lip, my thoughts unclear about the mixed signals I got from Brad. Was Cam right about Brad's trustworthiness, or was my erstwhile boyfriend jealous? Erstwhile because I hadn't heard from him since he saw Travis kiss me after the game.

She placed her hand over mine. "What's wrong?"

Forcing a smile, I shrugged. "Nothing important." Nothing except how I'd feel if Cam decided to drop me. I knew my heart would hurt, but didn't know if I should take a chance on him or cut my losses before I passed the "too late" line. Dang. Cam had gotten under my skin but good.

Coffee and pastry claimed our attention. Besides Cam, I wondered about the arguments I'd overheard Nicole holding with someone. Had she been angry with her father, or had she been speaking with another?

"Maggie, did you tell Dirk about the arguments you overheard?" Great minds and all that. Though I couldn't read Katie's and Ginger's minds the way they did each other, I loved that the three of us were close enough to think alike. Or possibly we were friends because we had similar thought patterns. Either way worked for me.

"Yes, I did, but you know what the political structure is like in this town." The mayor's daughter would be canonized never cauterized.

"And did you let Tom Jenkins in on the conversations?"

"Yep. I got the feeling the only reason I'm not behind bars is they want an airtight case before making an arrest. The mayor avoids embarrassment like a dieter shuns carbs."

"Well, if the cops don't act on the lead, you know what'll happen, right?"

"I get jail time."

"Nope." She smiled. "The Triple Threat Trio will get on the case."

Somehow I didn't feel reassured.

Chapter Eleven

My hand curled around the phone I'd moved away from my ear in disbelief. Returning the handset to my hearing organ, I repeated what Katie had just announced. "Travis argued with Nicole the morning she died? Are you serious?"

"As Ginger's bank account." Katie's irreverent way of telling me she had serious information. Ginger's inheritance from her grandparents had not been paltry, and her investors had significantly increased the original amount. "How did you find out?"

"I have my ways."

Katie excelled in coercion mode. I almost felt sorry for Dirk. But no doubt she'd gotten the information from the grapevine, not Dirk.

"Yeah, Travis and Nicole made the mistake of arguing over coffee at Java the Hutt. Stupid, right? Like no one would notice in there?" I could picture Katie rubbing her hands together with glee. For years, Nicole, Travis too, had been on her list of people she wanted to kick out of the gene pool.

"Really. Where'd you hear this?"

"Where else? The grapevine. What, did you think Dirk would share information? Not that I haven't been working on him."

"Uh, huh. Katie, I don't want you getting in trouble with Dirk over me."

"Oh, that's not how I get in trouble with Dirk. Hang on a sec."

I heard the sound of a cap hitting a solid surface, then water pouring into a glass. After a short silence, Katie came back on the line.

"That's better. Hot in here. I needed a quick sip."

"I thought Dirk would've broken you of that drink-everything-in-sight habit by now." Another thought hit me. "He's not listening to us, is he?"

"No, he's not here."

I heard the sound of a glass hitting the table.

"Wait a minute. I know what's happening. You've got it bad, Katie."

A long silence was broken with a snort. "Yep. My mouth goes dry just thinking about the man."

The last had sounded like a grumble, but I knew better. Even with a bad haircut, Dirk had women craning their necks for a second look when he passed. I couldn't imagine sleeping with the guy. Not that I would, given Katie's a friend. And, hands down, I preferred Cam. Even though he hadn't answered my calls.

"Anyway, the reason I phoned is to tell you about Travis and Nicole's argument."

"Did anyone hear their words?"

"They kept their voices down, but everyone in the place knew the two were pissed off with each other. So, of course they tried to overhear the prom queen and king."

Her intonation told me the two appellations weren't meant as favorable.

"So, tell me already."

"Nicole said something about investments and

promises. Travis said he'd never guaranteed a return."

That fit in with the arguments I'd overheard at the reunion breakfast and the dinner. Nicole had been involved in something up to her still firm chinny-chin-chin. Along with Travis and his investment expertise. So how did Clarice fit into the picture? Because this new information made me realize Clarice's unexpected bank balance meant her murder could tie in with Nicole's. Travis had hit Granville Falls in time to be responsible for either or both killings. Well, so had other former classmates, but none with such clear connections.

"Maggie? You there?"

"Yeah."

"You don't sound, um, I don't know. So hot."

"I'm fine." I drew in a deep breath. "Really. Does Dirk know?"

"Yep. Don't worry. He hasn't found the key yet, but it lies with our classmates."

I caught my breath. Intellectually I understood someone I knew had killed both women. Accepting that knowledge was something else. "And you know this, how?"

"I have my ways."

Glad I wouldn't be on the receiving end of her devious interrogation technique, I planned a get together with her and Ginger. I planned on calling Cam after work until he answered or driving to his house and knocking until he opened the door. We'd both been acting like children. Enough avoidance.

With no Nicole badmouthing me, my Monday afternoon schedule had filled. I hung up and left for the spa.

Standing beside Dolores, I watched my last client noodle-walk out the door. "So how are you doing?"

She shook her head. "I'd spoken with Nicole that morning. She sounded fine." Dolores swallowed. "We were headed for the outlet mall this weekend." Her voice rose on the last words.

I drew her into a hug. "I'm so sorry for you."

She clung to me, her body shaking. That's when I finally understood at a gut level that two people my age, from my high school class, had died violently. I'd been so worried about my innocence I hadn't spared a thought for the losses suffered by Clarice and Nicole's friends and family. And I'd thought my rich clients were self-absorbed. I felt lower than dirt. The dirt that's buried deep, not the top soil.

Dolores backed away, wiping her tears with the heels of her hands. "Don't pay attention to me. I shouldn't have blubbered all over you, especially after the way Nicole treated you."

What could I say? Don't worry about it?

Nicole and I would never have been best buds, but this reunion had done one good thing. It'd made me realize even the rich and surgically augmented beautiful have problems. Someday I'd forgive Nicole, but I'd never forget her ill treatment of me. The two were not incompatible.

"Dolores, are you sure you want me here? I'm the number one suspect on the gossip loop, right?"

Her tear-filled gaze met mine. "You stay. I'm not going to lose two friends over this. There's no way in hell you killed either N-nicole or Clarice."

She always hiccupped right before sounding full-blown sobs. I enfolded Dolores in a hug until she stopped crying then cleaned up my massage space. I threw my laundry bag filled with sheets, blankets and face rest covers into the back of my car. Turning to reenter the Lotus Spa's back door for my handbag and a sack of CDs, I ran into a solid wall of muscle.

Travis.

I scrambled in my haste, backing away with no dignity and less grace. He grabbed my arms, holding on until I steadied.

"Maggie. We need to talk." His face held no smile, and his eyes were dark, unreadable. This man—my long ago former boyfriend—looked like a stranger.

"I don't think so." My voice sounded like a squeaky gate. I cleared my throat. "I mean I'm on my way out. I really don't have time right now."

"Please give me a minute. Believe me, Maggie. I've heard what people are saying. We fought, yeah, but I didn't kill Nicole. Hell, I didn't kill Clarice, either."

I stepped back, whether in disbelief of gossip or in self-defense, I couldn't say. No one had given me the low-down on Travis, and now I wondered why not. Travis stood expectantly, but I didn't second his declaration of innocence.

"Then why didn't you leave yesterday with the rest of the class who live elsewhere?"

His Adam's apple moved and he stared at me. "I, uh, agreed to help the cops with their investigation."

Meaning they'd "suggested" he stay in town. He reached for me again, grabbing my arms before I could move.

"I swear, Maggie, I'm not a murderer." His voice turned bitter. "Other stuff, yeah, but I didn't kill anyone."

"Other stuff? What have you done?"

He shook his head. "You don't want to know."

"Oh, I think I do. You can't expect me to believe your word, can you?"

Travis hung his head. "I guess not. But Maggie, I'm sorry about what happened senior year. You believe me about that, right? I mean, once you decided to stay home and give up the scholarship, we'd have broken up anyway."

My body shook. I couldn't believe he'd apologize then emotionally bodyslam me. "My mother had a fatal illness, and you know my dad left before I hit kindergarten. Would you have left your sick mother alone and gone off for a good time?"

His expression crumbled. Travis rubbed his neck. "I'm sorry, Maggie. I didn't think."

"Were you considering backstabbing Nicole instead this time, or did the knife get buried in her back by accident?"

His face turned white. He shook his head. "I didn't. I swear I didn't."

I studied his expression. The truth in his eyes told me what I needed to know. Or else I thought his expression looked innocent. Over the last fifteen years, Travis could have perfected the art of lying with a straight face. I just didn't know.

My heart told me Travis didn't kill anyone. My brain proclaimed him a liar. He was a cheat, if I'd correctly understood what he'd inferred earlier. But a murderer?

I believed—hoped—his essential goodness, the spirit that had originally drawn me in, remained. Buried maybe, but still there.

My heart won the discussion. I saw the moment he understood I believed in his innocence. He grabbed my hand, entwining our fingers.

"So will you give me a chance, Maggie? Can we at least be friends again?"

I looked down and realized a fact I'd never noticed in our years together as a couple. My short fingers barely fit around his larger ones. His nails were buffed while mine were ragged, even after the manicure I'd gotten last week.

"Our hands don't fit, Travis. They never did."

His brow wrinkled.

"What I mean, Travis, is that we don't belong together. Not in high school, not now, not in the future." My heart grew lighter with the words. "You are a special memory for me. Let's keep it that way."

He opened his mouth and I thought he might try arguing the point until a small smile crept across his face. "Special memory, huh?"

"Yeah."

We exchanged a long look.

"At least let me kiss you goodbye." Travis bent his head and covered my lips with his. I hadn't felt the old spark for him after the basketball game, and it hadn't lit me up today, either.

A door creaking open caught my attention. I broke the kiss and turned. Cam stood at the spa's back entrance, Dolores at his shoulder.

Travis coughed. "I, um, Maggie and I were just saying goodbye."

Cam's jaw tightened. "Looked like hello to me."

Chapter Twelve

Travis took off before I realized he'd left my side. My attention had remained on Cam. Cam and his big brown eyes filled with accusation.

"Are you getting back together with that douche bag?"

His tight expression made my breath stutter. "N-no." I inhaled. "You heard. Travis said good-bye."

"That clinch looked too hot for a kiss-off. And that flash suit wants his hands on you."

Flash suit? He must mean Brad. As if gorgeous clothes decorating a well-developed body made up for his personality.

The door clicked closed with Dolores inside. Her disappearance reminded me that Cam had been out of sight and contact since the game.

"Oh, and you have the right to say something about it, why?" I almost stamped my foot to discharge my sudden anger. Instead, my hands clenched. "After stomping off mad yesterday? Not answering your phone or returning my messages?"

He crowded my space. My fists hit my hips. Good thing, given my need to slug the man. I kept my hands where they couldn't get into trouble. "Well? Got any answers, big boy?"

He pulled me into an embrace so tight I panicked for a moment. I struggled to pull back, breathe, anything that would help me find control. Cam loosened his hold and lifted my chin.

"Here's my answer." He lowered his head and laid on a kiss that sent shivers down my body. Way too soon, he pulled back. "Got any more questions?"

Katie had warned me about men who used kisses to avoid answering. I finally understood what she'd meant about pulling up the big girl panties and pursuing replies. My underwear wanted off and to hell with the conversation. With a sigh, I leaned back in his arms.

"Yes, I do. Why didn't you return my calls? No, wait. What I want to know is how you could think I'd be interested in Travis? Do you think I'd share a special night with you then dump you? What the hell is going through that blond-haired head of yours?"

He leaned forward. I flattened my palms against his chest. "Nuh uh. You won't sidetrack me with a kiss. Answers or nothing."

His forehead leaned against mine. "I got ticked off yesterday, and we had a heavy work load today. I found you as soon as I could."

"Without calling first and wearing a scowl."

"Yeah, well, I didn't expect to see you making out with numb nuts in the parking lot. We had a fight just yesterday, for cripes sake. Then there you are, in a clinch with jerk face."

His jealousy flattered my ego on one hand and exasperated the hell of me on the other. The annoying hand had become the upper one. I stepped back. "So it's all right for you to act like a child, reacting before you know the facts." I inhaled through my nose, battling my rising temper.

"I'm not a kid. Six years younger than you. So

what?"

"Closer to seven, but that's not the point." I shook my head. "You act so young sometimes, like pouting instead of talking with me." I decided I wouldn't mention my own recent detours into childish behavior.

"I wasn't pouting." He grasped my upper arms. "Okay, I'll own up. I saw green, okay? I wanted to pound the guy for kissing my woman." He pulled me closer.

"Why won't you admit I'm your man? Because age doesn't mean diddly, not now, not ever. Only this matters."

His voice held a hint of desperation, and I wondered how I'd misread his protectiveness for envy. My maturity looked more in question than his.

His lips covered mine with light pressure. He nipped and soothed and nibbled his way around my jaw. Cam's fingertips caressed my cheekbones and over my forehead. The closer he got to my ear, the harder I found standing.

"So what do you say?" He followed up his whisper with teeth tugging on my ear lobe.

"Say?" With difficulty, I pulled at my big girl pants again. "I say this isn't the best place for this conversation."

His hands, rubbing my back in small circles, stilled. "You were back here with a man who could have killed two of your classmates. Alone. Now you're saying the employee parking lot isn't the place for a conversation?"

My lips tightened into a straight line. I tried to push away, but Cam held me tight. "Idiot. My nipples could cut glass and you've got an erection the size of Texas."

I slapped my palm against his chest. "I meant we should move to a more private location, but now I don't think so."

His grip loosened. I slid to the side. "What do you mean?"

"Travis didn't kill Clarice or Nicole."

He snorted, sounding like the bull I remembered from my uncle's farm. "Right."

"I'm sure." Well, pretty sure. Travis had fooled me before.

"You're going to believe a pretty face over the evidence?" He rubbed my back. I moved away.

"No, I'm going to believe in an old friend."

"Someone you haven't seen in fifteen years. Over me." He sounded incredulous.

"Maybe."

We studied each other for a long moment.

"We're doing it again," he said. "Going into stand-off mode instead of talking."

I sighed. "You're right. You know, you're pretty smart for a youngster."

"Youngster? I'll show you youngster." He pulled me against his body, his erection proving his point. Pun intended.

After a few minutes of taking evidence, I ducked back into the spa, picked up my belongings, and headed for home. Cam followed me. Purely for security reasons, of course.

****

The next morning, I finally picked up all the newspapers that lay strewn over my front porch. Reading the headlines made me sorry I'd bothered carrying the newsprint inside. I should have walked the rolled-up garbage right to the trash bin.

"School Is Murder."

"Mayor Slams Police Inaction in Daughter's Murder."

"Mayor Forms Reunion Murder Task Force."

Cam walked in, his hair still wet from the shower. "Hey, woman. Wanna fight again so we can have more make-up sex? You were so hot I'm still steaming. I almost took a cold shower to cool off."

Our gazes met. He pulled me against his chest. "What's wrong?"

I held up that morning's paper. "Police Expect Reunion Murders Arrest Soon." The sub heading read "Local Businesswoman Lead Suspect."

Nuzzling my neck, he whispered in my ear. "Stop worrying. They'll find the guy."

I didn't believe him. Although I hadn't been named in the article, everyone would know the identity of the "unnamed businesswoman." Dolores wouldn't be happy. Damned if I did or didn't, I packed massage supplies for the day and left my bag at the door.

Cam drew on his shirt then grabbed me in a tight hug. "I'm on your side. Always."

I threw my arms around his neck and held on while he used his lips and tongue to reassure me. His heart beat steady and sure against mine. Unsure what I'd done to deserve this man, I gave thanks for his presence and strength.

I broke the clinch, knowing if I didn't, we'd both be late for work. My hand cupped his jaw. "You are one special man, you know that?"

"I'm nothing without you."

We lingered over our parting kiss. I wore a silly-ass grin all the way across town.

Dolores met me at the Lotus Spa's door with a hug and full schedule. Apparently, the women of Granville Falls either believed in my innocence or they'd decided to live dangerously by having a massage under the hands of a suspected murderer. Either way, making my monthly expenses looked a done deal with cash left over. Phew. Now I just had to worry about avoiding jail and affording my lawyer. Piece of cake.

My attention fully engaged in my clients, the morning sped past, and my lunch break arrived. I headed for the small room that doubled as storage and a place for employees to rest their feet. The space didn't boast relaxing art or soft furniture like the spa's reception area, but still offered comfort away from the chatter.

Dolores stuck her head in the room. "How're you doing, Maggie?"

Returning her question with one of my own on her emotional state sat on my tongue, but I could see she grasped her composure with a tenuous hold. Humor seemed a good response.

"I'm thinking of asking for a private room at the Share Shack. That'll make it easier to transfer information. No delay in leaving here and driving there. Almost as fast as the Internet."

"Yeah, and as accurate."

I laughed. "The Web could take pointers on validating information from our neighbors."

"You know I can't let you do that. I'd go out of business pretty quick if Denise added massage. And I don't mind second-hand news." The expression on Dolores's face moved from amused to sad in a nanosecond.

Jumping up, I gathered her into a hug. "You've had a rough time, haven't you?" I swallowed. "Are you sure you want me here right now? I mean, I hope you aren't taking a hit on my account."

"Are you kidding me? Bookings are up." She stepped back and wiped her tears with the back of her hand. "No, I haven't changed my mind." She shook her head. "It's nothing."

I put my arm around her shoulders. "It's something. What's wrong?"

Dolores shuddered. "No one knows this."

I closed the door after checking the hallway. Turning back, I patted her shoulder in what felt like an ineffectual gesture. "I won't say anything if you want to tell me."

Her lips turned up at the corners. "I know. I trust you, Maggie." She took a deep breath. "It's about the spa."

Only my body's automatic processes kept my heart pumping. "What about the spa?" My voice sounded hushed.

"Nicole." I saw her swallow. "I'd been in a spot a few months ago and Nicole helped me out. She didn't want anyone to know, but she invested in my business." Dolores sniffed. "We're partners. Were partners."

I'm no lawyer, but I thought I saw the problem. "Did you have a partnership agreement?"

She shook her head. "I had one drawn up, but for some reason, Nicole wouldn't sign. She said she'd give me the money and I could pay it back over time, no interest."

My hand stopped rubbing her back. "So you're

saying she never signed papers?" That sounded odd, especially because Nicole prided herself on her no-nonsense business head. Her real estate business handled most of the town's residential sales, along with commercial land. She'd been a partner in several of the new McMansion subdivisions that had attracted Charlotte commuters. Still, Nicole had mentioned needing money to leave town. Perhaps her deals had left her land poor.

I felt Dolores inhale. "Nicole said something about wanting no record of the transaction. Later, after I kept pushing, she said she'd signed the agreement, but I never got a copy."

"And now you don't know if she signed for real. And if she did, if the agreement is with her estate papers."

She nodded. "Or what will happen if her f-father calls the loan."

"Can he do that?" I rapidly considered the options. "You sure as shoot don't want him as any kind of partner."

"God, no." She shrugged. "I haven't checked my original copy. Guess I need to do that."

I hugged her again. "Don't worry. Most partnership agreements have a clause in case of death." Geez, Maggie. Put a foot in. "I'm sorry. I didn't mean—"

She finally hugged me back. "It's okay. We're both in a tight spot, aren't we?" She released me. "Ah, Maggie. Now it's my turn to apologize."

"Forget it. You spoke nothing but the truth."

Dolores left and I sat down to finish my lunch, my appetite diminished. Without the spa booking for me, I'd have an even harder time making ends meet.

Besides that, according to Dolores, Nicole had a sweet side I'd never seen or even suspected. Were her hard-assed, man-stealing ways a cover or her preferred way of dealing with most people? Could her generosity with one close friend make up for her general bitchiness toward everyone else? Did the conversations I'd overheard highlight Nicole as a victim or co-criminal?

I didn't know, and my unwanted mean girl genes complained about having to change my long-standing opinion of a life-long enemy. Or to consider that perhaps Nicole's fatal backstabbing had deprived her of a chance for change.

Chapter Thirteen

"I don't care if Nicole helped Dolores." Katie rubbed her forehead with one finger. "She had an angle." She raised her hand, palm out. "I vote Nicole was up to her stuck-up nose in whatever is going on."

"Katie, Nicole had friends. She couldn't have been all bad."

From Katie's narrowed eyes, I knew she didn't agree with Ginger's assessment, but she kept quiet. Me? I mulled. Thoughts, not wine.

Katie plucked at a crease in her slacks. "Why would Nicole invest money with no record? Sounds funky. We need to get to the bottom of the murders and their cause."

"I agree," I said. "But how? Dirk will have your head if you interfere and I've got no clue how to investigate anything besides a knotted muscle. Besides, Tom Jenkins has a detective working for him. I'm not putting you two in danger."

Ginger chimed in. "Yeah, and after our last investigation, Katie, I sure don't want another chase through a cemetery at midnight." She caught my gaze. "But I'll do what it takes so you don't get railroaded." She leaned over and put her hand on mine. "Count me in on any T-Cube action."

"The other thing we need answers about is how Clarice made her money and where it went." Katie snorted. "No way she consulted at the level she earned. Everyone in town would know it." She caught Ginger's eye. "You hear anything?"

Ginger shook her head.

Pointing to me, Katie asked, "You?"

I joined Ginger in the head shaking.

"Don't you think that's odd? And worth looking into?"

Sounded like a starting point. "How?"

Katie smiled. "I have a hankering for some truffles."

Ginger snapped her fingers. "Of course."

It took me a few seconds but then I tumbled to their grins. The Chocolate Fix.

My keys jangled when I grabbed them. "I'll drive. If we hurry, we'll get there before Mona closes."

We made it downtown in record time. Entering the small storefront, I breathed in the scent that would have revived the *Princess Bride's* "mostly dead" hero, Westley. Chocolate, coffee, and cocoa combined with a hint of apple cider, cinnamon, and other spices. All in one place.

The late afternoon sun slanted in the large front window, spilling over the square ceramic floor tiles. We strode directly to the glass-fronted display cases holding a selection of truffles.

"Ladies, good to see you this afternoon." Mona placed one hand on the counter, the other on her waist. Her generous curves proved if the store's aroma hadn't, that she created rich chocolate and didn't stint on the taste testing. "What can I get for you? I'm still offering triple chocolate malts, but I'm morphing into my fall drink specials. Take your pick. Or did you just come in for chocolates?"

Her smile indicated she knew we'd come for more than a sugar high. Lifted eyebrows seemed to ask why we'd waited so long.

"Mona, we want it all." Katie held up a finger. "The best chocolate anywhere." She held up another digit. "Something to drink." Adding a third finger she said, "Information."

"Not necessarily in that order." Ginger said. "Or only for those reasons. You know we can't go for more than a week without a visit."

Mona laughed. "I can't deny two of my best customers. Let's start with truffles."

We placed our orders and settled at the small table closest to the counter.

Mona quickly put together our drinks and arranged truffles on a square white plate, carting them to our table on a tray. We made short work of sorting out our confections while Mona flipped the lock and her "Open" sign to "Closed." She slid into the chair beside me.

Tangy key lime and white chocolate flavors exploded in my mouth. I'd barely emitted the requisite groan of pleasure before Katie asked her first question. "So, Mona, what do you know about Nicole Polk? Or Clarice Dawkins?"

She'd caught Mona in the process of popping half a small truffle into her mouth. Mona licked her fingers then chewed. I sipped at my mocha latte and shifted in my chair.

"Clarice never came in, and I didn't know Nicole well. She wasn't a regular customer, but she did order gift boxes for customers on occasion. Never came in, always ordered over the phone." She snorted. "Some people are afraid they'll put on weight if they walk through the door."

Given the heady aroma of fresh ground cocoa beans, I could understand. Not that I'd agree. Ever.

"Did she order for anyone lately?"

Her forehead wrinkled then smoothed. "Father's Day. Plus she closed on a house or two last month." Mona sipped her coffee. "I did appreciate her including my chocolates in her thank you baskets she gave people who bought through her agency. I know I picked up new customers."

Ginger reached for a truffle. "You'd have gotten those customers anyway. You make the best chocolate in North Carolina."

Mona smiled. "Thanks, Ginger." Her expression turned serious. "No matter what people said about Nicole behind her back, she aced brokering sales and she always supported local businesses."

"She had to," Katie said. "Her father is the mayor."

"No, it's not that. I think Nicole wanted Granville Falls to prosper and she planned on riding to the top along with the town."

"We're already overrun with Charlotte transplants." Katie scowled. "I liked us better before we grew. Nicole's daddy hasn't done this town any favors."

Ginger smirked. "But if GFPD hadn't needed another detective, you'd never have met Dirk."

Katie stuffed a truffle in her mouth.

Mona watched the byplay, her lips twitching. "Anyway, I didn't know Nicole very well, except for seeing her around town. But if it's gossip you're after, I can give you plenty of that."

Katie leaned forward. "Did you hear anything about Nicole and Clarice? Or rather, Clarice's husband? Or what kind of consulting Clarice did?"

Mona held up her hand, palm outward. "Don't hold back your questions." She smiled and swallowed a sip of coffee. "If Clarice did any kind of consulting, no one in town knew about it. She spent a lot of time volunteering and hanging with the country club set. You know, the movers and shakers." Mona put air quotes around the last three words.

Katie opened her mouth but Mona continued without interruption.

"Yes, I heard that Nicole went after Clarice's husband, and the smart word is that she caught him. Not only in bed but also in business. He joined the group building that last subdivision along with Nicole and another partner. No one knows the silent partner's identity, but he or she provided the big project money."

"What does Clarice's husband do?"

Mona shrugged. "Investment banker? Corporate lawyer? I'm not too sure. Some kind of crook."

Her crook comment reminded me that Mona hadn't told anyone much about her past other than her old hippie history. She'd never moved past her dislike of big business, even when approached with Chocolate Fix franchise opportunities. Bankers and lawyers would definitely fit her definition of law-breakers. I wondered if she'd hit on the murderer's motive.

"We know she talked about her investment and wanting results." Ginger didn't mention I'd overheard the conversations.

Katie nodded. "She told us off at the reunion

dinner. She said that she couldn't wait to leave town after her investments paid off."

Mona turned to me. "And didn't you tell Nicole that it would have been better if she were dead?"

I squirmed. "Um, yes, kind of." I inhaled and blew a long breath. "I told her she should have died rather than Clarice." I knew the words by heart. I'd been replaying them since they popped out of my mouth.

"I'd heard that. Too bad you said it in front of the sexy cop." She played with her coffee spoon. "I also heard that your ex-boyfriend told Nicole to watch her butt."

So much had happened in the last few days that I didn't recall. Travis's words hadn't made it to my memory banks. Probably because I didn't want anything more of his in there.

Ginger tapped her fingernails. "No, I don't think that's right." Her face scrunched in thought. "He said something else." She raised her hands, palms up. "I don't recall, but I'm pretty sure Travis didn't say she should watch her butt."

"I'll ask Dirk if anyone mentioned the exchange."

"No, Katie, let me ask Cam first," I blurted. "You don't need trouble with Dirk."

She grinned. "I told you. That's not how I get in trouble with him."

Ginger put her hand over Katie's. "Let Maggie ask. I have a feeling Cam sees more than he lets on." She removed her hand. "Besides, Maggie needs to take some action." She smiled at me. "Right?"

I nodded. Someone had implicated me in two murders, and I wanted them nailed to the prison cell wall. So much for my nice girl genes.

Mona finished her coffee and placed her empty mug on the tray. We took her hint and piled our empty dishes alongside hers before standing.

She looked each of us in the eye. "Be careful you three. Greed is a strong motivator. Could be another motive behind the killings, but I suspect money. Whoever murdered your two classmates won't be shy about killing again."

We walked to the entrance. After hugs all around, she shut and locked the door behind us.

My stomach churned. I had strong friends who believed in my innocence, a top lawyer racking up fees I'd never pay off without a huge lottery win, and too many questions to let me sleep a solid eight hours.

"Okay, so thanks to Mona we've got a direction, right?"

Katie's question cut through my absorption. "I'll speak with Cam tonight. See what he remembers about the interaction between Travis and Nicole at the dinner."

Ginger said, "I'll contact the country club set and ask about Clarice."

We looked at Katie.

"And I'll check with my boss, Jim, about Nicole's real estate dealings. He'll know the rumors about her latest subdivision plans."

My stomach calmed. Maybe I'd get some sleep tonight after all.

****

Cam waited on my porch. Looked like I'd get lucky. You know, about finding out what he remembered of Travis's comments to Nicole. Although his bodacious bod had my girl parts humming, I still craved sleep.

I drew closer and saw a pizza box on the seat next to him, an open can of beer in his hand. "Hey, Big Guy. Whatcha doin'? No chairs available at the inn?"

He put down his beer, stood and pulled me into a tight embrace. "Thought you'd like dinner in tonight." He toed a small cooler at his feet. "Dessert."

"My kind of man." I massaged his neck with my hands. His lips were another matter, and massaging just wouldn't do when I could sip, nip, and lick them instead.

Untold minutes later, I stepped back and unlocked the door. "I'm glad you're here." I helped him cart the food and set the table. After I had inhaled one slice and eyed a second, I felt my blood sugar climb. Sure, chocolate is a food group, but I'd needed protein.

"I planned on calling you."

"Oh, yeah? Booty call?" He waggled his eyebrows and grinned. "My answer is yes."

I didn't know whether to roll my eyes or laugh, so I did both. "Actually, I need some information first."

"First?" He licked his lips. "Sounds promising."

I leaned across the table toward him. "Do you remember, last Saturday night, when Travis and Nicole joined our table?"

He looked like he'd bit into a lemon instead of the banana peppers that dotted the pizza. "I'm afraid I do." He eyed me. "How important is your question?"

"Important."

He set his pizza onto his plate and sat up straight. "Hit me."

"Right before Nicole left the table, Travis said something to her about watching her butt. Do you remember exactly what he said?"

Cam shrugged. "Sure. He didn't tell her to watch her butt. Travis said her investments might bite her in the butt." He rubbed his chin. "That's as close as I can remember."

"You're sure?"

He smoothed his thumb over my cheek, brushing off wayward crumbs. "Yep, caught my attention. He'd looked on his way to a champion drunk until the catfight started. Then he almost appeared sober. When he made the comment, he meant his words, no mistake. Of course, that didn't last long."

Cam was right. Travis had hit the booze from the time he sat down. After Nicole left, his imbibing increased. Ginger told me that after Cam and I left, two of his former basketball team buddies dragged Travis home so he didn't pass out at the table.

"Is that it? Your only question? Because I like cold pizza and hot women." He smiled. "Not necessarily in that order, you understand."

I blinked. He'd caught me cogitating on the investments biting Nicole statement. I didn't doubt Cam had gotten it right. "Wait a minute. You think we had a cat fight with Nicole?"

He grinned. "You hadn't gotten to the hair pulling yet, but it sure looked like a cat fight."

"So you like cat fights, hmm?" I bent toward him, and his eyes went to my cleavage. "Hey, Tom Cat. Wanna spat with me?"

His pupils turned big and dark. He put a hand behind my head, yanking me toward him. Our kiss began hot then turned feral.

I heard clattering and knew he'd pushed our dinner

off the table. He moved fast, rounding the wooden slab, and encircling me from behind. Hot, wet kisses covered the back of my neck, his teeth scraping my skin. His large hands cupped my breasts.

I fought to regain just one small thought process. Instead of saying, "let's move to the bedroom," I heard my husky whisper voice another sentiment. "Hurry. Here. Now."

Thank the heavens he listened. I knew my idea of "tabling the matter" had undergone a radical definition. And "doggie style" would forever be renamed in favor of felines.

Chapter Fourteen

Cam and I shared a hot and heavy night, so once again I didn't get my needed eight hours. Not that I cared. I could run on love fumes, no problem.

I toddled into the spa and another full day's appointments. Knowing life's unpredictability I gave every client my best massage. I'd made my rent and then some this month, but I had an ongoing practice to maintain. I hoped.

When I left the room at my lunch break, I saw that Dolores had tacked a note to my door. My new door. Dolores had created a space for me after Liz returned from the beach. Even though the crime scene tape had been taken down, emotionally I couldn't return to my original room. Dolores had also lent me her old table. After checking with the cops, I'd tossed the table Clarice had died upon. No amount of spiritual cleansing would make a difference.

The note read, "Katie and Ginger, lunch at the Chocolate Fix today." Mona didn't serve sandwiches, so unless my friends brought me food, I'd be running on love and sugar until supper.

They waited for me, waving as I walked in the door. Their gestures made it clear I should get a move on. Katie looked smug while Ginger couldn't sit still. I felt my pulse pick up and slid into a chair across from them.

"You won't believe what I learned," Ginger said. "I can't wait to tell you."

"I can't wait, either," Katie added. "She wouldn't say anything until you got here. I was ready to drag you out of the spa by your hair." She turned to face Ginger. "You'd better go first before you vibrate out of the chair."

"Maggie should eat."

"Just for that, I'm making you wait."

I defused the standoff. "I'll go first. Cam heard the exchange between Travis and Nicole." I repeated what he'd told me the night before. "So it sounds as if she had more going on than we suspected."

"I'll say she did." Katie leaned forward and lowered her voice. "My boss knows everything about construction in town, including the underhanded stuff." She held up one hand palm out. "Not that he's involved in that crap, but it's a small town."

We all nodded. Sometimes Granville Falls felt too little for comfort.

"Anyway, he'd heard Nicole had entered into some shady dealings."

She looked over her shoulder and we joined her in scanning the room. No one paid us attention, but that meant nothing. Some of the older ladies sitting across the shop had ears like bats.

Katie's voice dropped to just above a whisper. "Jim said Nicole worked in cahoots with her daddy. Seems Papa the Mayor helped her cut a few zoning and code corners when she built her subdivision. Jim heard he stepped on some toes in the planning department."

Ginger's eyebrows rose and mine resided just below the ceiling.

"I knew Nicole had bad blood. I can't figure how she killed Clarice, but I still nominate her for the honors." Katie sat back with a satisfied smirk.

Ginger's eyebrows dropped when her forehead wrinkled. "You think Nicole killed Clarice? That doesn't make sense. Wouldn't the same person have murdered both women? Besides, she'd stayed in another room, fixing her face after getting a massage. You know how relaxed Maggie's work leaves you."

Katie waved her hand and Ginger's comments away. "Who's to say Nicole didn't do it? I'm keeping her on my bad guy list until proven only half-assed bitchy. Jim told me the construction on those houses sucks. If you stand in the basement looking up, you'll see more nails sticking out into air than driven into floor joists. The floors will buckle. If Daddy Dearest didn't push the inspectors to overlook problems, how did her houses pass? She was always bad news."

I turned to Ginger. "So does any of this information tie in with what you learned about Clarice?"

She shifted in her seat, looking like she performed a chair dance.

"I'm still gathering facts, but it appears Clarice's goody two-shoes reputation had tarnished." She reached into her bag and pulled out a notebook. "I took notes after the meetings so no one knows why I asked questions."

She flipped open the cover. "Clarice told varying stories about her business. Some people thought she'd inherited a bunch of money from a great aunt in New York, while others had the impression she ran a small consulting firm. And I also heard stories that she and her husband invested together, and he funneled money to her for tax purposes."

Katie tapped the table with her fingertip. "Smart cookie. I'd never have suspected her of deceit. She was always so quiet in school."

"Yep," I agreed. "Docile. When I remember Clarice, I think of lambs or bunnies. The odd-ball group, like Brad." Hadn't Clarice been a part of that clique? I seemed to remember she had.

"Hey, even mice have teeth," Katie reminded us. "I'm not revising my opinion of Nicole, but maybe those two were more alike than we realized."

"I'll say." Ginger leaned in. "Because some folks heard Clarice's last investment had been, guess where?" She raised her eyebrows but didn't wait for our answers. "Nicole's subdivision."

"Clarice as mystery partner?" Katie snorted. "No way. I don't believe that. Clarice hated Nicole. Remember that bit about her husband being seduced by our Prom Queen?"

Ginger flipped a few pages, marking a spot with her forefinger. "Katie's right. Here's Clarice's husband listed as an investor. The amount doesn't match what Nicole needed for startup. Tax papers listed a corporation as the developer, but I couldn't find the company listed on the Dow."

Sometimes I forgot that Ginger isn't just a pretty face. After her husband Rob lost a chunk of her inheritance with bad investments, Ginger taught herself to read and follow the financial markets. By all accounts, her skills were acknowledged as top-notch.

"I'm still researching, but I'd say it's a dummy corporation. Most likely one of a series of holding companies designed to hide the money's origins. It may take a while, but I'll keep digging."

Katie rubbed her forehead. "This is starting to sound serious. Land swindles, do you think? Insider trading? Money laundering?"

Ginger shook her head. "Probably more along the lines of tax evasion with a hint of political corruption."

My stomach muscles cramped. "Either way, we should just let the cops handle the investigation. I don't want anything bad happening to you two."

Katie stared at me as if she could reassure me with her gaze alone. "I'll let Dirk know the scuttlebutt without naming names, but you saw the papers, right? He's getting pressured to make an arrest. He may not have time to follow all leads."

Ginger placed her hand over mine. "We've faced worse. At least no one is shooting at us."

"Hush your mouth." Katie nudged her friend. "If you'd all listened to me, we could've nabbed the bad girl right away, but nooo. Nobody believed me then."

Ginger and I prudently refrained from answering.

"We've got your back, Maggie. We won't retreat from a little politics as usual."

I wished Katie's comment made me feel safe and secure but it didn't. Katie's reminder of my proximity to a jail cell gave me the shakes. Ginger reached across the table and enfolded me in a hug. Katie isn't a hugger, but I felt her concern and support wrap around me when she patted my hand.

"If anyone can find the information, it's you, Ginger."

I agreed with Katie's declaration. Ginger looks like a model but she's got a spine and brains. "So where are we? How can I help?"

"First, you can eat this salad I brought for you." Ginger reached into her bag and pulled out a covered bowl.

Katie pushed a paper wrapped roll toward me. "I got Dora to make you a sub sandwich."

Mona approached carrying a tray. "I thought you might like chocolate for your conference."

Stunned, I looked at the women who had my back.

"Ah, crap." Katie's forehead crinkled. "If you cry, I'm leaving."

Ginger shook her head. "I thought you were working on a kinder, gentler Katie?"

"A work of art takes time."

I choked out a laugh. Wiping away a stray tear or two, I caught Mona's attention. "Do you mind if I eat this here? Will you get in trouble with the Health Department?"

Mona smiled and handed me a stack of napkins. "The department manager's wife is one of my best customers." She waved a hand. "Just don't make this your regular lunch stop."

My chest tightened. "Thanks, and I won't."

I tucked the sandwich into my bag. "Thanks, Katie. I'll save this for my next break. I'm working late tonight." Then I started on the salad, hoping I didn't spill on my blouse as I scarfed an excellent mixture that deserved more of my attention.

The bell above the shop door dinged. We looked up as one and saw Brad. He spotted us, took a few steps in our direction then veered to the counter when Mona greeted him.

Katie's eyes narrowed. "What's he doing here? I

mean it's not like Brad is a chocoholic. He didn't even eat the dessert at dinner on Friday." She tapped her finger on the table. "When I asked him if he liked cheesecake, he told me that sugar is poison and he wouldn't "sully his temple." As if."

Ginger choked back a laugh. "He does have a pretty impressive temple these days. Did you offer to eat his dessert for him?"

"Ha. Funny."

"An aversion to sugar is no reason to distrust a man, Katie."

"Brad told me he's visiting his mother this week," I chimed in.

"Yeah?" Katie's voice held a hint of suspicion. "Why would a man whose mom complains he's never home for long spend two weeks here now? I get why he came for the reunion, I guess." She glanced over her shoulder to the counter. "He just looks and acts so different. It's mind boggling, but how much has he changed inside?"

Shooting another look toward Brad still talking with Mona, I contemplated the misperceptions caused when you hold onto the past. My thoughts were interrupted when Brad, who'd misinterpreted my blind musings as interest, approached us.

"Ladies. Are you having a nice lunch?"

I murmured an answer, my reflections still centered elsewhere. All contemplation ended when Brad asked Katie a question.

"So, any news on the murders? I was surprised the cops didn't make the whole class stay."

Katie threw me a glance I couldn't interpret. "They've got everyone's contact information. Unless you're a millionaire with Swiss bank accounts and multiple off-shore properties, anyone not living off the grid is easily found."

"I guess you're right," he answered. "Still, with the mayor's daughter involved, I'd have thought an arrest would be made the first day."

Katie's clipped out an answer. "Sure, maybe on television. Sometimes finding the real killer takes longer."

He tilted his head. "I'm glad the police are being careful." He caught my gaze. "I'd hate for the wrong person to get convicted."

My breath caught. I shoved my hands under the table to hide my shaking.

Ginger stepped in to what felt like a developing fray. "So would we."

"Perhaps all that's needed is a little incentive."

I wrinkled my forehead. My forehead did that a lot, lately. I figured I could plant spring crops in the furrows my frowns left. That'd be the only way I'd get fresh veggies in prison. Shaking off dread I asked, "Incentive?"

"A reward. Cash for information."

Katie's expression remained stoic, but I sensed her interest. "What kind of reward?"

He looked at the ceiling. "I'm thinking $25,000 for information leading to an arrest."

"Why would you spend that kind of money, Brad?" Katie's voice held an edge. "Do you think the police aren't doing their jobs?"

His answer came soft-voiced but tense. "I guess you didn't know, or maybe you don't remember. Clarice dated my friend, Sam Sievers, back in the day.

She treated me nice when a lot of other people didn't. I want her killer caught."

My face warmed, and I wondered how I'd acted toward Brad. I couldn't remember, or rather, had chosen amnesia about those years.

"In case it matters, you three never made me feel bad. I always liked you girls."

Thankful he hadn't mentioned his crush on me, I blew out a breath. My stomach churned. This reunion had made me realize that I'd been a shallow, unconcerned person for a lot of years. It's hell facing your actions and finding you lacked human decency.

Brad held up a small Chocolate Fix bag. "Anyway, I just stopped by to pick up chocolates for my mom. She loves this place."

"So how long are you in town, Brad?" Katie's tone held a smidgen of challenge. Apparently his reasons for offering a reward hadn't softened her attitude toward his inferred slap at GFPD.

"A few more days. I hope I'll see you around. Have a nice day." He strode for the door and left without a backward glance.

"Really, Katie." Ginger shook her head. "Why did you berate him? He's offering help."

Katie tapped a fingernail against her teeth, her attention still on the entrance. "Moi?" She faced Ginger. "I get the feeling he's only talking reward for his own benefit."

I stood. "Sorry. If I don't leave right now, I'll be late for my next massage appointment."

A series of hugs and heartfelt thanks followed, then I raced back to the spa. As I readied my table for my next client, I pondered the scene with Brad. The incongruity of Sad to now Bad Brad still had my thoughts spinning. I couldn't help feeling Brad's motives for putting up a reward were rooted in his high school years. This was his chance to play big man on campus and live down his Sad Brad nickname.

Did we ever outgrow our teen-age angst?

If I survived this situation unscathed, I'd run the next time the past reared its ugly head.

Chapter Fifteen

I dragged my exhausted self home, grabbed the sandwich I hadn't finished earlier, and polished it off. Cam was stopping by, and I figured a quick shower would energize me. At least I hoped it would.

As I slipped out of the bathroom, a towel wrapping my hair, I heard the phone ringing.

Thinking Cam called, I answered without looking at caller ID. "Hey, I sure hope you can make it tonight. I need a foot rub. Maybe more."

Silence. Dang. "Cam?"

"No, but I wish I were."

"Oh, uh, hi, Travis. What's up?"

"Nothing that will get relieved on this end without you, that's for sure."

I caught myself smiling then shrugged and grinned. It felt good hearing a horny teenager's comment from an old boyfriend. His gibe reminded me of when he'd teased me about my determined virginity while we'd dated.

"I'm so not going there."

"You sure know how to hurt a guy."

My smile faded. "So. You called, why?"

"Just wanted to see how you're doing." His tone dropped. "I'm glad you're still answering your phone in person."

"Yeah, me too."

"Anything new on the case?"

"Not officially. I haven't been called in for more questioning, which I guess is a good thing." My fatigue and our renewed camaraderie had me blurting my concerns. "It's just, I don't know, I think there's more to these murders than anyone is seeing."

"Really? Why's that?"

I shouldn't have said more, but my internal censor had shut down. "Well, Katie and Ginger are helping me look into some gossip we've heard. It seems that Clarice had been involved with Nicole somehow."

"Maggie, no. Don't go there."

The alarm I heard in his voice caught my attention. "No worries, Travis. Katie dates the lead investigator. She'll keep him informed." If not, I figured Dirk had his own ways of ensuring Katie stayed straight.

"I'm not kidding, Maggie. Two people have been murdered. Our classmates. People we knew for years. I'd hate to attend your funeral, too."

"Nothing bad will happen from checking out a few rumors, but if I don't...well, I could end up in jail."

I heard his soft breathing in the pause before he answered. "I'd hate that, too, Maggie."

"Look, I know you're involved in the financial community and this is a small state for all that it reaches from the Atlantic to the Appalachians. Would you do me the favor of letting me—or the investigator—know if you hear anything pertinent about Nicole or Clarice? They had connections with big money investors, we think."

"You know I believe you're innocent, Maggie, but you should be careful where you poke around."

I heard his long exhale. "What do you know?"

"Nothing. Not really. Whenever big money is involved, things can get dicey. Promise me you'll stop investigating on your own."

"Why won't you help me?"

"Warning you off is the best help I can give." He sighed then silence fell. "I'll tell you whatever information I can find, for old time's sake, okay?"

"Great. Thanks, Travis. I appreciate your help."

"Just be careful. Big money plays by different rules than the rest of us."

"I will. Thanks again."

Hanging up, I turned and saw Cam leaning against the living room doorway. He frowned. "When were you going to tell me?"

My foggy brained warned me to stall. "Tell you what?"

"Travis. You told me that ended years ago and you hadn't picked it up again. Did I get that wrong? 'Cause I don't share girlfriends."

"Cam, no. I wouldn't two-time you." Not like his last girlfriend who shredded his heart when she broke their engagement last spring and eloped with another man. All in the same night. I'd heard she'd even kept his ring.

"So he just happened to call."

"That's right. I hadn't heard from him after he left the spa. I'm as surprised as you are." I figured I'd better not mention I'd thought the call came from Cam and my subsequent request for a foot rub. I thought we'd gotten past his jealousy, but it remained understandable, given his romantic history.

His jaw loosened but his eyes still sent a glare that could refrigerate a food warehouse. "You shouldn't leave the door open with a murderer loose in town."

"I did?"

He nodded. "When you didn't answer, I tried the door." His Adam's apple moved as he swallowed. "I worry about you. Even more after what I heard you say on the phone."

Thinking back to the foot rub comment, I wondered when he'd arrived. "How much did you hear?"

His eyes narrowed. "You and the girls. Looking into rumors. Knowing you're hanging with the Demonic Duo is enough to give any man a heart attack. I saw Katie's kitchen after the murderer hit it." He shook his head. "But then you ask your ex-boyfriend for help. What the hell Mags? Aren't you in enough trouble already? Am I not smart enough to help you?"

"If I don't help myself, I'll end up giving the warden weekly chair massages. Not my idea of running a business."

"You wouldn't have money worries if you'd move in with me."

What did he say?

"Did you hear me? I said I want you to move in with me."

His direct look told me he didn't joke, but I hadn't heard those sweet words that would get me jumping in his lap. Not to mention I still had niggling concerns about our age difference. I closed my mouth and swallowed my pique.

"So you hear me talking on the phone with a male friend and now you want me to move in with you?" I planted my hands on my hips. "Talk about trust. Not."

"I trust you. It's the guys you attended school with

that I don't like. Plus, I hate that you worry about everything. I can make life better for you. Let me help."

"Kind of like a brother, is that it?"

"Brother? Where the hell did you get that idea?" He moved closer. "I don't have sibling thoughts about you."

He placed his hands on my shoulders and gently shook. "I love, love you, you goof ball."

My mind raced, but I choked on an honest response. Instead, I voiced the first coherent words that made it through the blur. "Did you lock the door behind you?"

"Damn right I did."

"Good." I eliminated the tiny distance between us, wrapping my arms around his waist. Tugging him closer, I stood on tiptoe and covered his lips with mine. "I'm sorry."

His forehead wrinkled. "Sorry? Why?"

"For making you worry."

"So you'll move in with me?"

I eased back. "I don't think that's a good idea right now."

"Right now, or right ever?" He ran his fingertips over my cheek, and his thumb pressed against my lips. "I want you safe. What I heard you say on the phone, well, I think you're headed into danger. That scares me, Mags."

We exchanged long looks.

"I know you don't like Travis, but I think he's innocent. Well, not totally innocent."

"You're in over your head."

"It's my life."

"Yeah, you've made that clear."

"Cam, it makes no sense for me to move in with you when my next residence might be a cot at the North Carolina Correctional Institution for Women."

"You're innocent. Tell Dirk what you know, or suspect, about Travis. Make sure Katie tells him what the three of you have figured out. Promise me you'll call him tomorrow."

"Katie is bringing Dirk up to speed. And we haven't learned much, yet." Not that the rumor mill wouldn't give us the information we needed, and soon, or Ginger missed her mark. "Besides, I think someone murdered Nicole and Clarice for personal reasons. We didn't share social connections, so the killer won't mess with me."

He stared at me until what I'd just said penetrated my thickness. The killer had messed with me all too well. First by using my work area for his dirty deed with Clarice, then implicating me in Nicole's death.

"Yeah, okay, so I just said something dumb." I rethought my position. "Still, I think the first murder could have been a mistake, or someone taking advantage of circumstances. I'd been set up for Nicole's death because it made sense—I was already a suspect."

"Yeah, you keep thinking that someone—a killer—doesn't have it in for you." He clenched his fists. "You're safe here all by yourself when the sociopath comes to call."

Put like that, I wanted to crawl up next to him and leave without packing. Just grab a toothbrush and go. But I also knew that I'd been framed for two murders and no bodyguard, regardless how delicious, could have prevented that happening. I needed room to move, and living with Cam would hamper investigation. No psychic sense needed to infer that truth.

I hugged Cam, my hands moving up his back to his shoulders. "You are a special man. I appreciate you, but I can't live with you, not until I'm cleared of murder."

"Then let me help you. I can't just stand by and do nothing."

I rubbed his shoulders. "Oh, I can think of something I need right now. And you're my pick for the job."

His lips quirked. "Oh, yeah? You want me for my body again, right? Why not my mind? Huh. Never thought I'd say that."

After our laughter faded, I pulled his head down for a kiss. "Actually, I could use a foot rub and a snuggle session. I'm beat."

That's when Cam proved he's not just a pretty face and gorgeous body. I fell asleep spooned in the arms of a man who rubbed my feet like a professional. Finally, I got a full night's sleep. And more of my niggling concerns about our relationship melted away.

****

"Promise me you'll think about my offer." Cam's hands moved over my stomach and hips early the next morning. If he moved a little lower, I'd agree to anything. Even without coffee first.

"Okay." My body relaxed under his continued ministrations.

Movement stopped. "I mean it, Maggie. You'd be safer living with me."

I lay there comfortable and disinclined toward argument but the truth loomed clear. If a murderer wanted to hurt me, I couldn't really stop him. Besides, as long as I remained the number one suspect, I counted as too important to knock off.

We performed our morning ablutions, detoured several times because of proximity. My rental house had just one teeny bathroom. After a sexy bout in the shower and another caused by toweling each other off, Cam finally left for work. Not that I felt sorry about the delays. They just provided more food for thought.

I was falling in love, and the fact scared the bejeezus out of me.

****

I didn't have enough on my mind or plate, so when I opened the door on my way out, I received another jolt. Detectives Dirk Johnson and Matt Pulaski stood on my porch.

"Dirk. Matt."

Dirk answered for the pair. "Maggie. May we come in?"

As if I'd hold a conversation with two cops on my front porch when my neighbors were salivating for the next installment of the "is Maggie guilty" saga. "Sure." I stood aside and they filed past.

We got settled, and although Matt unobtrusively sniffed the coffee-scented air, I didn't offer them java. They hadn't come on a social call.

With a sigh, Matt pulled out his notebook and a pen. He settled into my sole club chair. Dirk perched alongside me on the couch.

"So should I call my lawyer?" I held myself stiff at the edge of the cushion.

"Maggie, relax, we just need clarification on some prior testimony. Go ahead and call your lawyer. We can wait."

Maybe they had time to spare but I already ran late. My shoulders dropped and I inhaled. Even though Jenkins had counseled me to phone no matter what, it sounded like they were just checking my prior statement. I may as well get past their questions sooner than later. I couldn't think of anything I hadn't already told them.

"Go ahead. For now."

"We," his hand gesture indicated he and Matt "are hoping you have information you haven't shared."

I shook my head. "I don't know anything I haven't told you. Besides, I thought you were here to check prior testimony."

Dirk remained still, watching me. "No new information gathered through the grape vine? I hope you're not holding back evidence, Maggie. If so, you'd have an obstruction of justice charge to answer."

I thought for a moment. "I have nothing further to say." Jenkins would be proud of me. Damn it all. I really should have called Tom, regardless of piling up more billable hours I couldn't pay.

"Okay, I have a question not related to the case. You don't have to answer. What do you know about the politics in this town?"

My shoulders crept up toward my ears. "The mayor gets his way with the City Council because he's broadened the tax base by luring the Charlotte commuters here. Old timers aren't too happy with him. They preferred Granville Falls as a smaller and friendlier town." I shrugged. "What do you mean?"

Dirk leaned toward me. "Everyone knows you, Katie, and Ginger are asking questions. By the time Katie clued me in on your actions, I'd already had multiple calls from the mayor's secretary, his deputy, and the man himself. Along with a slew of concerned citizens."

He rubbed one finger across his forehead. "They all wanted to know when "those girls" had been deputized."

I shrank against the couch back. "We just wanted to help."

His calm demeanor dropped away. "What the hell are you women thinking? You're in over your heads. There's a murderer loose in town and he's targeted you, Maggie." His eyes narrowed. "Either that, or you've done a hellava job convincing your friends you aren't a killer."

All the emotions I'd been repressing flooded my body. Combined they resulted in anger. "Well, dang, thanks for the vote of confidence."

He nodded at Matt. "We're investigating all aspects of this case in depth. If you learn something about the murders, tell your attorney or us as soon as possible. We need to hear all the facts. Even the gossip."

"We didn't mean to make your job more difficult, it's just...well, we know you're under pressure and the mayor's on your case." I caught his gaze. "I don't want to go to jail, Dirk." My head spun with the course of this conversation.

"You don't give the GFPD much credit, Maggie."

My face heated.

Dirk pinned me with a glare. "We're looking for a killer or killers." Dirk rubbed his forehead with his fingers. "A case could be made that you're asking questions to divert suspicion."

Dang. His words made me feel guilty, and I knew I hadn't committed murder. I gulped.

"How many times do I have to tell you that I didn't kill anyone?"

Dirk's quiet answer sent my pulse wild. "Words don't make it so, Maggie."

Dirk and Mat's impassive faces stared back at me. I had no friends in the room. For all I knew, they'd cave to pressure and come for me when I least expected their arrival. I stiffened my spine. Asking questions around town, no matter how dangerous, could be my only chance of survival.

"Nothing I've heard sounds like checking prior testimony. I'll be calling Tom Jenkins now."

Dirk stood and Matt copied his lead. "No need. We're leaving."

They stomped out, and I concentrated on pulling in oxygen. I waited until I saw them pull out, then grabbed my day's supplies and headed for the door on shaky legs.

Either I waited for the cops' help or I took my life, and possibly my friends' lives, in my hands. I didn't like either option. I suddenly felt like a catnip toy between the paws of a bloodthirsty feline.

Then I opened the door on another surprise.

Chapter Sixteen

"So Dirk stopped by to put the fear of God in you, right? I figured he'd show after Brad suggested a reward for information yesterday." Katie handed me a tall coffee to go from Java the Hutt then stepped across my threshold. "Did you call Tom Jenkins?"

I grabbed the cardboard container like manna from Heaven. "Fear of God? No, they were checking my prior statement. I didn't think I needed my lawyer for that." I wouldn't tell her about Dirk's implied threats, but the additional stress had my stomach churning. "Aren't you supposed to be at work?"

Katie plopped onto the couch in the same spot Dirk had occupied a few minutes earlier. "I've got to run out to a job site and drop off updated plans. Lucky me, huh? Thought I'd stop by before you left for work."

"And you just happened to arrive right after Dirk left?"

"Yeah, my timing could use some work, huh?" She grinned. "So what did he tell you?"

"We're in over our heads."

"Guess Dirk forgot I starred on the swim team in high school."

Tears pooled in my eyes. I blinked them back. "You're my star now and always. You and Ginger. I don't know what I'd do without your friendship."

Katie squirmed. She still hadn't learned to accept

compliments very well, but at least she hadn't begun blustering.

"Speaking of Ginger, wait until you hear what she discovered." She rubbed her hands together and cackled.

"Why do I get the feeling you didn't share this info with Dirk?"

She sipped from her cup, savoring the buildup, "Actually, I did, earlier today. He's having someone check it out." She leaned toward me. "I wouldn't suppress information that will prove your innocence. If Dirk doesn't listen, we'll check the stories ourselves."

Given my recent discussion with her lover, I knew he wanted every tidbit he could get.

"Anyway, you know how Brad's mom is always bragging about her son?"

"Yeah, but we always figured she built him up to make herself feel better. It couldn't have been easy having a known dweeb for a son and a former jock as an ex-husband." I'd felt sorry for the drab woman who'd driven her nerdy offspring to school every day. Well, as sorry as a shallow teenager can be on the few occasions her situation occurred to me. "Besides, how were we to know she told the truth?"

"The reason why Brad succeeded remains in question. Anyway, Ginger investigated." Katie stopped and sipped.

"And?"

She wiggled her eyebrows. "Brad's the CFO all right, but industry rumors have him on the outs with his boss and the BCI Directors." She sipped coffee again but I held my piece.

"Brad," she stretched out his name, "is involved

with some high level corporate politics. Sounds like he's fighting for his career."

"He is? I thought he said he—" I thought for a moment. "He said a deal had gotten hot. I just assumed he'd meant for his current company."

"Ginger couldn't get details, but Rob told her he'd heard Brad had gotten in trouble at MIT. He may not have dropped out." She grinned. "I'll bet I know what kind of trouble. Hacking." She returned her attention to her coffee.

I sat quietly, figuring Katie deserved her spotlight time. Plus, my thoughts were tumbling like a class full of toddlers learning to somersault.

She placed her cup on the table. "Anyway, Brad landed a job at BCI right out of school."

"So he's never worked anywhere else?" I sat back. "Ten years or more at the same job and now he's in jeopardy."

"Yeah, so new, improved Brad may disappoint his mama after all."

"She'd never be disappointed. He's her reason for living. Remember when the cops showed at school and took him home? After his father beat up his mother and left town?"

Katie sobered. "I'd forgotten. For a long time, her only public appearances were when Brad played varsity golf."

While I'd missed my father after he ran out, I sure wouldn't have wanted that scenario. My attention returned to the present.

"So Cam nailed it. Brad does have a secret. His success may be short lived."

"True. But then, we all have information we don't

share, and corporations are one big mass of backstabbing politics. Get more than one materialistic person in a room and things will head for hell sooner than later. Those guys and their golden parachutes always end up on their feet."

"But a position loss? Wouldn't that be a big ego blow?"

She shrugged. "Ginger has a hunch that Brad acted as Nicole's secret investment partner. Could be Brad is branching out. If he leaves BCI on his own, his ego doesn't take a hit."

"What? No way. Nicole made Brad's life miserable in high school. Don't you remember? She had her stupid jock boyfriends stuff him into a locker. And they'd knock over his lunch trays, trip him, all that bullying stuff."

Katie leaned forward. "What better way to kick bully butt? Come back a successful CFO and lord it over your enemies."

"But, Katie, he's offered a reward for information in Clarice's murder. If anything, he's a good guy."

"Then who played Nicole's investor? And Clarice. Who paid her consulting fees? Travis? You? We know someone in our class is a murderer. The way people are getting knocked off, our suspect list has narrowed and I don't want you convicted for crimes you didn't commit."

I swallowed my tongue. Not really, but it sure felt that way.

"One thing I've learned from Dirk is trust no one until they've proven themselves and their motives. I know you're not a killer. That leaves two known options and the always popular "person or persons unknown.""""

"Will you talk this over with Dirk?"

"Cop A-hole? The man who told me they have financial experts on the case and Ginger should go back to baking cookies?"

That explained why Katie hadn't come in while Dirk and Matt were here.

"You mean the man who told me to "stop the girl detective act?" That he had the case under control?"

Okay. Her rant had some strength.

"The man who made fun of my Demonic Duo cape?" Her voice level and tone rose. "Who threatened to put me in jail along with my friends for our own good?"

Uh oh. I bit back my own anger. No way could I tell Katie that Dirk had intimated he thought I could be a murderer.

"The man I may never put out for again? That man?"

"Um."

"I see you get the picture."

"Yes, well—"

"Well, damn nothing. I say Brad is in this up to the knot on his silk tie. And I'm not so sure Travis is an innocent bystander. His whole forgiveness act just hit me wrong. He says he's missed you but doesn't bother calling or writing for fifteen years." She snorted and threw up her hands.

Katie's suppositions had been proven right before. Plus, her observations made me uncomfortable. But so far she'd been wrong about Nicole being a murderer. I couldn't reconcile the changes in Brad, but that didn't make him, or Travis, killers. I kept my doubts to myself, though.

I flexed my hands. "Okay. What next?"

"Keep Brad from leaving town before a certain cop who-is-too-stupid-to-live has a chance to arrest him."

"Not a problem. Brad said he's here all week visiting his mom."

"That's what he told *you*. The truth is something else again. He's got money, undoubtedly a passport, and reason to run. I say we do a stakeout. My cape is in the car."

"And I say you should call Dirk." I finished off my coffee. I'd rather call a snake, but I kept my mouth shut about Dirk's earlier visit.

"Matt. I'm too pissed off to call he-who-must-be-obeyed."

I figured Dirk had grounds for anger too, but wouldn't open that subject for discussion. Especially because I currently agreed with her.

"I'm not calling him. You want to report our *crazy ideas*, go ahead." She stood and paced. Katie mumbled in a loud whisper about "jerks," "no appreciation" and various deprecations I knew referred to Dirk. I almost felt sorry for him then scotched my sympathy. He'd lost my good will earlier today. The man needed help dismounting from his high horse and Katie figured as the one to assist.

"Maybe we should call Tom Jenkins instead." At least he appeared anchored on my side. Even though my billable hours would rise through the stratosphere with the extra work involved in following this lead.

Katie's eyes narrowed. "I get the feeling something happened here that you're not telling me." She put one hand on her hip. "Just what exactly did my live-in jerk face say?"

"Nothing, nothing. It's just that I prefer not facing an angry cop, that's all."

"Hmph."

"I'm with you. They can follow their own leads." I set my empty cup down.

"I'm glad you agree." She made shooing motions with her hands. "Let's go. You can ride to the job site with me." She wiggled her eyebrows. "Cam is waiting for the new plans." Katie grinned. "I know he'll be happy to see you riding sexy shotgun."

"Your plans for revenge on the male race starring my, uh, Cam can wait. Take out your anger on your real target tonight. I'm already running late." I checked the clock and realized I'd have to rush.

"Spoil sport. By the way," she examined her cuticles, "I overheard Cam talking with someone this morning. He wants to keep you safe." She added air quotes around the last word.

"What?" I glanced at the clock and knew I didn't have time for a detour. "He has no right."

"Macho, alpha man." Katie sang and gave a hip shake as she misquoted the disco tune lyrics.

"I don't have time for this." Grabbing my supplies bag and purse, I snagged my keys from the table. "Let's meet for drinks tonight. I have a feeling I'll need a super-sized alcoholic something."

Katie matched my race for the door. "Sounds good. I'll call you later."

We took off in opposite directions, but I figured we'd be united in spirit today. And over alcohol tonight.

I stewed over Cam's behind-my-back plans to an

unknown someone as I drove. The fact that he didn't try hiding his conversation from Katie told me Cam had my safety in mind. Still, he needed to back off. Heavy dating—okay, and plenty of hot sex—didn't make him my hus—*gulp*—keeper. I shied from completing the word I'd almost thought.

Dolores met me at the door. "I worried something had happened to you." She glanced at her wristwatch. "You're usually earlier than this. Is something—"

Wisely remembering she had clients eavesdropping in her adjoining waiting area, Dolores helped me carry my bags. We stopped outside my room.

"I'll tell you later, I promise." We hugged. "It's all good."

I hoped she wouldn't feel my tense muscles and know I lied.

"Your first appointment is in fifteen minutes, with a full morning, then nothing after one o'clock," she said.

I called Tom Jenkins after my second client had left. He had court, so I left a message relating Ginger's research. With the billing clock running, I omitted Katie's suspicions about Brad's potential link to Nicole. I wondered if Clarice's business could be the key we'd all overlooked.

My inability to help myself weighed on my mind through the rest of my appointments. Mrs. Sievers, my last client, waited for my ministrations. At least I excelled with my job. I pasted on a smile and knocked before entering.

Mrs. Sievers, the mother of my classmate Sam, had kept her youthful appearance. Her pleasant looks didn't reflect her reputation as a shrewd observer. She turned her head and eyed me.

"You look surprisingly relaxed for a murder suspect."

My smile slipped, and I forced my expression back into happy lines. "Good afternoon, Mrs. Sievers. Thanks for making an appointment with me."

Determined to keep our interaction on a professional basis, I continued before she could voice another word. "Do you have a particular ache bothering you today?"

"Yes. My heart aches over those murders. I've been having nightmares about my Sammy winding up dead. You know he dated Clarice in high school, right?" She shivered.

My hand hovered over the massage oil pump bottle attached at my belt. "I had a reminder of that fact just yesterday. Are you having pain anywhere? Your shoulders? Lower back?"

I struggled to keep her on track for a massage, knowing she'd settle in when ready. Meanwhile, my thoughts flew to high school years. Sam Sievers had hung with the "out" crowd, the misfits who found each other through some odd sense of recognition and banded together at lunch and on the bus. Brad and Sam had befriended each other. I wondered if their mothers had done the same.

"Oh, I don't pay aches any attention. At my age, if I noticed them all I'd never get anything done. Just do your thing, dearie."

"You aren't old, Mrs. Sievers." I knew she ran marathons and took Zumba.

I folded back the sheet and warmed oil in my palms before applying it to her back. Some clients liked silence, others were chatterers. Mrs. Sievers fell into the latter group.

"Yes, Sammy wasn't the only one who had a crush on Clarice, poor thing."

I didn't know who the "poor thing" was so didn't comment.

"Sammy and Clarice dated junior year before she dumped him." She sniffed. "At the time, I could have killed her for the hurt she put on my poor boy."

My hands stilled for a moment.

Mrs. Sievers chuckled. "No, I didn't kill Clarice sixteen years after the fact. She did Sammy a favor. He went off to college, found a lovely girl and they gave me two gorgeous grandchildren. Still happily married too."

"That's great. Too bad I didn't see Sam and his wife at the reunion dinner." I found a knot under her shoulder blades and applied pressure.

"Umm. He probably sat with his friends all night. My Sammy is loyal to a fault." She lay quietly. "No, Clarice was bad news back then and she acted no better now. It's a shame she was murdered, though. Bless her heart. Carrying on with Brad Crosby, and her a married woman." She tsked. "And that husband of hers. Talk about two peas in a pod. He and Nicole Polk were flirting and flaunting all over town. "

Her muscles eased and I moved to her neck.

She took a deep breath and exhaled. "Yes, Arabella and I worried about Brad getting sucked in by that hussy."

"Arabella? Is that Mrs. Crosby?"

"Yes, and a better mother you wouldn't find anywhere. Outside of me, of course." She laughed then gasped when I hit a tender spot. "Please, dearie, a lighter touch."

"Sorry, Mrs. Sievers, you've got a toxin build up there. I'll warn you in advance if I find another." I resumed working on her muscles and waited for her to continue. I knew she would.

"I guess that's a polite way of telling me I talk at the wrong times." She chuckled with the noise muffled but identifiable.

"No, I just want you to enjoy your experience."

"Where did I leave off? Right. Arabella. Well, we've had some conversations the last several months. Arabella knew Clarice chased after Brad for his money. You did know he's done well for himself in California?"

"I assumed that once he returned for the reunion. Brad and I weren't really friends."

"That's too bad. He had a big crush on you in school."

I finished with her back, replaced the sheet there and uncovered her left leg.

"Yes, Arabella had hopes you'd notice her boy, but of course, that didn't happen. You were going with that basketball star Travis Knowles, right?"

As if she needed a reminder. This woman tracked social groupings in her head the way a computer sorted data. Her memory didn't break down or get lost in electrical outages, either.

Making a noncommittal noise, I continued with the massage.

"Getting back to Brad, I often thought he'd make a good doctor, but he went into business instead."

I made the expected response. "Doctor?"

"Oh, my, yes. Brad's father taught him to use a knife. When he wasn't on that computer, he studied anatomy and life sciences. He had the makings of a good surgeon. I know because my brother is a doctor."

Before I could absorb that comment, she'd moved on.

"Arabella mentioned she heard her son tell that woman, Clarice, he wanted his money."

I waited for her to continue, but knowing she had a captive audience, Mrs. Sievers stopped speaking and waited. A classic bait and switch move.

"Is this pressure working for you, Mrs. Sievers?"

"Yes." She waited.

After a short pause, I gave in. "Huh. Wonder what Brad meant by wanting his money? Do you think he did business with her?"

She snorted. "Funny business if you ask me. He told Arabella he'd lent Clarice start-up money for a project."

I moved to her right leg after tucking the sheet around her completed extremity.

"That doesn't sound odd. One old friend helping another."

She turned her head. "Sending her a stream of money every month for her consulting services? Consulting on what? Who does business like that?"

"How did she know? Mrs. Crosby, I mean."

"Oh, Arabella could give a bat lessons in hearing. She knew something smelled and listened in on Brad's conversations." Mrs. Sievers grunted when I worked on a tight thigh muscle. I applied pain relief gel and moved on.

"Well, I told Arabella she could relax once he gets

back to California tonight. Both our boys will be safe."

"Tonight?" Only my years of practice kept my hands steady with even pressure. Otherwise I might have broken the poor lady's leg.

"I know. It's so sad. Arabella rarely sees her son and now he's leaving a few days early. Something about a South American business merger opportunity." She stilled. "Ecuador? Paraguay? I can't remember. But she's proud of his success."

Mrs. Sievers switched to discussing her grandchildren. I had to hold her on the table or she'd have slipped off to grab her wallet-sized photo album. Only my promise to look through all the pictures after her massage ended kept her in place. That, and the fact that she'd finally relaxed into loose muscles.

Once again I found myself operating on automatic pilot while a client lay on my table. My thoughts flew from point-to-point.

Brad planned on leaving early. Tonight and headed for South America. One of those countries had no extradition treaty with the U.S., but which one? And would Brad really head there or to some other country?

Just as importantly, a link had been established between Brad and Clarice. He'd been funneling her money, and a jump to his silent partnership with Nicole didn't take much imagination. Plus he knew how to use knives and had studied anatomy. Sad Brad had graduated to the big time, and I hoped, to the big house. The one with guards and bars. Because even though I hadn't fully believed Katie, once again I was sure she'd nailed the criminal's identity.

After an extra fifteen minutes oohing and aahing over some really darling towheads, I ushered Mrs.

Sievers to the door.

"Dearie, you did me a world of good. I'll be back for another massage. Well, unless you get arrested." She turned back from the exit. "Not that I think you capable of murder, bless your heart." She patted my cheek. "You don't have it in you, sweetie."

I thanked her and grabbed my phone and Matt's business card. This lead had come unbidden, and was too important to leave as a voice mail. "Come on, come on, answer."

A damn message instruction. After this whole mess ended, I'd find out why the town's detectives never answered their damn phones when you needed them.

My second call to Tom Jenkins also resulted in a message because he had a court appearance. I debated calling 9-1-1, but responding to gossip wouldn't be considered their emergency.

I dialed someone I knew would respond. "Katie, where's Dirk?"

"I'm not his mother," she sniffed. "Why?"

"It's important, and Matt's not answering his phone."

My tense tone must have alerted her. "Maggie, what's happened?"

"It's Brad. I just learned he's leaving tonight. Do you know if Dirk and Matt talked with him after you gave them Ginger's information?"

"We haven't spoken a word since last night."

Well, that explained a lot.

"Maggie, we need to act fast. Can you pick up Ginger? We'll have to follow him."

A noise at my door alerted me to Ginger standing in front of me. "She's here now."

"Ginger?"

"Yes, Ginger. How soon can you get away from work?"

"Give me fifteen, no twenty minutes. Let's meet on Pleasant at Fifth, around the corner from the Crosby home."

"Got it."

"Oh, and Maggie?"

"Yep."

"Don't forget your capes. The T-Cubes ride again."

Katie hung up and I looked at my phone before flipping it closed. "Capes?"

Ginger moved into the room. "Uh, oh. Capes? Had to be Katie on the phone. What trouble are we getting into now?"

"I'll tell you on the way."

Chapter Seventeen

Katie pulled alongside my car. She lowered her window. "Do you have your capes? I have a feeling we need all the luck we can get."

Ginger reached into her bag at her feet and removed neatly folded black vinyl. "I've got mine right here. Not that it'll stop bullets."

"Hey, I paid to have those gravestones fixed months ago." She glared at Ginger. "You sound too much like Dirk."

I held out a hand toward each woman, palm out. "Ladies, please. What's our plan?"

Ginger pointed a finger at a passing vehicle. "Well, if I'm not mistaken, we should be following that car. The one Brad's driving."

I looked over my shoulder and saw a black sedan with a man at the wheel. By the time he'd slowed for the stop sign a half block away, Katie had executed a Y-turn and swung in behind Brad. My car had a tight turning radius. I performed the maneuver quickly and got in line.

If the situation hadn't had serious implications, I'd have laughed at our resemblance to cruising Main Street as teens.

"Where do you think he's headed?" Ginger's voice held a tense edge. We were connected with Katie via cell phone.

Katie's voice came through the speaker clearly. "I'd say I-85 and the Charlotte airport, but that's just me."

My knuckles tightened around the steering wheel. "Don't follow too close, Katie. He couldn't have missed seeing us when he passed."

"Hey, we're just out for a drive. It's a nice day."

Thunder boomed overhead as dark clouds swirled. Ginger and I jumped when a wad of newspaper hit the windshield then flipped off.

I cleared my throat. "Uh, huh. Nice day for a drive."

"This next intersection should give us a clue. If he goes right, it's the airport." We could hear Katie whistling. "Crap. He's getting in the left lane. Must be headed for the mall."

A car cut us off, blocking our view of Katie's vehicle.

"Crap, crap! He just jumped into the right lane and I can't get over! Move over and follow him until I can catch up!"

I checked the mirror but had already begun swinging into the right lane. The driver behind us, who'd also been moving over, simultaneously slammed on his brakes and horn. I waved with my full hand instead of the single finger I thought he warranted. I mashed the accelerator. The maneuver kept us two cars back from Brad.

Ginger had watched Katie make the left turn. "That girl is crazy. No, she's driving me crazy."

"Is she following us? Did she make it through the light?"

"Yes, but don't ask me to describe how she did it."

Katie's voice sounded from the telephone speaker. "I can hear you two, you know."

I voiced my worries. "Now that we're all traveling in the same direction, we should try Matt or Dirk again. This guy probably killed two women. He won't worry about more victims if he can get out of the country."

"Agreed, Maggie. Katie? Should I call?"

After a slight pause, our friend in the other car answered. "I'll phone him. Even when he's royally ticked he takes my calls."

"Okay, I'll hang up. Call us back after you speak with Dirk, okay?"

"Yes ma'am, Commander Ginger."

Silence grew between us as we followed Brad. He made a circuitous trip through town and out into new subdivision country. I threw a quick glance to Ginger. "Where's he going?"

"I don't know and it worries me that Katie hasn't called back."

As if signaled, Ginger's phone rang. "Katie?"

"I think I know where he's headed."

My voice sounded strangled when I interrupted. "Did you reach Dirk?"

She didn't answer immediately, which worried me. "Yes. He told me everything is under control."

Ginger chimed in. "Katie, did he tell you to back off?"

"Uh, not in so many words."

Spasms hit my back. "I don't have a good feeling about this. We should pull over. Let the cops handle this. They can put out a no-flight order, can't they?"

Katie's voice boomed from the speakerphone. "Not if Brad has a fake passport and ID. Once he makes it to a non-extradition country, it's all over. We have to prevent him from reaching the airport just in case. At least try to slow him down." We heard her voice a curse word. "Now I know where he's going. That new subdivision of Nicole's is just down the road. I'm hanging up and calling Dirk."

Ginger squeaked, "Katie!"

Too late. Our connection ended.

"I'm calling Matt." Ginger dialed but received the same "leave a message" message I had. "There has to be a problem with Matt's phone. He always picks up."

A random thought occurred about Ginger's knowledge of Matt's phone habits. Then Katie's car made a sharp left turn between two elaborate entrance gates with the sign "Embassy Crest." I braked and followed at a slower speed.

We followed Brad along a zigzag course, past the skeletons of partially built houses sitting in the middle of large lots. "For Sale" signs flashed past like the old Burma Shave signs my grandfather had collected. Just as we all turned into a cul-de-sac, the dark clouds above us released a torrent of rain.

Even with the wipers at full speed, I couldn't see much past my car's hood. Rain beat down on the roof, making conversation difficult. One after the other, our cars halted in the dead end.

Ginger looked at me, her eyes huge. "I think we should lock the car doors."

"What if Katie needs help? We should join her, then lock the doors and call the cops again."

Our gazes moved to the window. The downpour slackened, the way it sometimes does in North Carolina. Storms here can hit hard and fast and end just as abruptly. We knew this storm could go in that direction or pick up in a heartbeat. Nodding to each other, we clambered from the car. Slipping and sliding on the mud that ran from the unfinished driveway on our right, we hurried toward Katie.

We'd almost arrived when we heard sirens approaching. Katie jumped out of her car, holding her cape over her head against the rain. I grinned at Ginger but her expression held horror, not relief.

Suddenly, a muscled arm caught me around the throat and yanked me backward. I choked, squeaking in protest. Not that I would have said much after I saw a gun with the barrel pointed at my two friends.

He motioned with his gun hand. "Move away." He jerked me by the throat again as he took two steps backward. Sirens wailed louder and blue strobe lights lit my friends' faces.

Brad yelled past my ear at Katie. "Tell the cops to back off." He punctuated his demand by pulling me closer. My feet slid but he held my upper body tight against his.

When my friends remained still, Brad shouted a follow-up command. "I know your cop boyfriend has pull. Do it."

The chilly mist following the earlier downpour turned to rain. Cold drops ricocheted off Brad, hitting my neck and shoulders. The rain intensified but was the least of my worries. Brad's stranglehold cut off my oxygen. I struggled to breathe. My vision blurred.

He shifted with his next step back. I pulled in as much air as I could. My feet hit a patch of mud and slid out from under me. Brad's arm slipped, and I felt him trying to regain his balance while maintaining his hold.

I fought for purchase and an opportunity to escape. Before I could gain my feet, my left arm caught Brad's. Our momentum threw us more off balance. I elbowed him hard then pushed against his chest. He went down but so did I. I sprawled across his legs, my hair in my eyes.

Blurred motion caught my attention, as a second man piled onto Brad's chest. Katie pulled me away from the struggling men skirmishing in the mud. I huddled shaking beside my car, pushing my sopping hair from my eyes. Ginger and Katie clustered with me, holding me tight.

That's when my heart stopped beating.

Cam. Oh, God. Cam fought with Brad. And the gun disappeared from sight. The weapon must have been between them.

I didn't know why Cam arrived. I wished we'd left Brad for the cops. But those weren't my first thoughts. No, I wanted to separate Cam from danger. Hold him. Keep him safe. Because he was my mine.

Cam and Brad didn't tussle long. They were quickly surrounded by police officers with guns and rifles drawn. I'd never been so happy to see an excess of armaments in my life.

Brad struggled briefly then stood still while being cuffed. As the officers turned him toward the car, he caught my eye.

"Nothing personal, Maggie. I had to make a business decision."

Matt stepped up and recited the Miranda warning.

The brawl, and my stint as a human shield, ended so quickly, I sat dazed. Cam staggered over and knelt before me. My cold palm on his dirty, overheated cheek and the question "How?" was all I could manage. Then an officer helped me stand and wrapped me in a blanket. He assisted me into one of the cruisers before blocking the door.

I leaned against the back of the seat and closed my eyes against the black spots dancing in my vision. My body felt like a rag doll. I couldn't have formed a cogent thought to save anyone's life.

Only one idea remained clear and bright. Never, ever, underestimate a dweeb.

Chapter Eighteen

The young cop who'd accompanied me jumped then ran when he heard his name bellowed. He left the squad car's door open. I was grateful because small spaces scared me sometimes.

I bunched the blanket under my chin. Unfortunately, the fleece didn't keep my teeth from chattering. An argument close by caught my attention.

"We talked this over. We have an agreement." Dirk held his hand out to Katie. "Give me that cape. Now."

Katie pulled her folded black vinyl morale booster tighter against her chest. "No. We're fine. This scenario doesn't apply under *your* rules. Nothing happened."

"Having a gun pointed at your chest doesn't count, right?" He wiggled his fingers in a "gimme" gesture. "I know that cape gives you false security. Enough."

"Brad grabbed Maggie as a human shield, not me. I knew you'd take him. Plus, I only agreed to stop being curious if my questions seemed too dangerous."

"You're not making your argument."

"I called you, didn't I?" Katie's chin jutted out.

"Yes, and it's a good thing you did."

Their gazes held. After a moment, she handed him her cherished plastic. Dirk reached for it but she maintained her grip. "I'm getting this back, right?"

He shook his head and the corners of his lips turned up. "We'll talk about it later."

They exchanged a look so heated I stopped shivering and glanced away. After a short tug-of-war, Dirk walked off with the cape under his arm.

A moment later, Katie nudged my shoulder. "Hey, how're you doing?"

Instead of answering her question I asked another. "How do you handle this?"

"Slide over." She joined me in the back seat.

She adjusted the blanket over my legs before speaking. "The yoga dude's death, well, that seemed easier because I didn't know him. Hadn't seen him before. Still, feeling his breath stop under my hands shook me up. The other stuff Ginger and I went through together, so we shared the trauma."

Katie inhaled deeply and blew a long breath. "But nothing about murder or crime is easy. Makes me appreciate Dirk that much more. I know he wants me safe. I'm just too stubborn to relinquish my say-so over me." She grinned. "Plus, the make-up sex rocks."

Their battle of wills, and Dirk's fishing expedition, made more sense now. He would always be a protector, and Katie came first.

Katie's aversion to surrendering her autonomy also made sense because it echoed mine.

My unwillingness for trusting Cam became clear. His age had little to do with my reluctance to accept him for my romantic partner. I'd been alone for so long—too long—that my real fear involved losing my independence. Yet Cam, even taking his jealousy into account, hadn't once kept me from doing what I wanted. He needed to keep me safe, but he didn't put me on a pedestal or in a golden cage.

I knew this insight, plus my emotional response

during Cam's fight with Brad, needed more attention than I could give sitting at a crime scene, huddled in a blanket. But the realization that I had found a man who wouldn't stifle me lifted my heart.

Katie rubbed her upper arms. "I feel naked without my crime fighter's cape. It's only because Brad got caught that I gave Dirk my good luck charm."

I figured her need for a talisman had disappeared once Dirk arrived on the scene, though she'd never admit that fact.

Matt approached and placed his hand on her shoulder. "Katie, Ginger asked me to find you. She could use your help."

"I'll get Ginger and drag her over here. We'll be right back." She covered my hand with hers. "This will all be over soon."

Katie moved away with Matt, and Cam took her place at the door. He took one look at my face and crawled into the car beside me. We sat so close we could have been Siamese Twins. He threw his arm over my shoulder. His presence felt safe. Reliable. My worries lessened.

His forehead wrinkled. "You okay?"

"Yes, but how did you get here?"

"I was with Dirk when Katie's call came in. He told me to stay put, but that wasn't happening. I followed them here."

I nodded. "You shouldn't have jumped Brad. He could have killed you." My voice shook.

"Nah. He's got gym muscles. I earned mine in construction. No comparison. The dude didn't have a chance."

"Still." I shook my head, and placed my hand on

his chest. "Don't ever do something so dumb-ass again."

His palm rested on my jaw. His fingers played with my earlobe. "What, I'm not supposed to protect the woman I love?" He shook his head. "You can't expect me to stand by while some shit-face has a gun to your head. Doesn't work that way."

"The cops were here. They'd have defused the situation."

"I stood closest. I knew I could take him." He shrugged. "No brainer."

I gathered a breath. "Cam, I love you. I don't want to lose you."

His fingers stilled. A smile lit his face. "I knew it! I knew you loved me too. Then why don't you—"

"Excuse me." Dirk stood at the door. "We need you both at the station for statements." He ran his hand through his hair. "You can follow us, or if you're not up to driving, ride along."

Ginger and Katie arrived on his heels.

He turned to them. "Katie, can you drive or do you want to ride with me?"

"I'll drive myself." Katie dropped her hands to her hips. "But I'm going home and changing first. You've got to book Brad and that'll take time. You can just wait for me."

"You know I will," Dirk said.

Ginger and I exchanged lip quirks. The intermittent rain started up again, this time as a heavy mist.

My recent declaration still rang in my ears. Emotion overwhelmed me along with an unwillingness to face my internal upheaval. Had I blurted my love because I'd been scared spitless? Or did I really want

Cam? I didn't know, and I needed time for thought.

"Ginger, do you mind riding with me?" My friend glanced at Cam then agreed.

Cam frowned. His shoulders hunched.

My breath hitched. He'd just put his life on the line and I was afraid of my feelings? Could I screw up any more?

Leaning into him I whispered, "I need dry clothes. So do you." I didn't have to force a smile. "And if you drive me home, they'll send a squad car after us when we don't show at the station. That could be embarrassing."

"Maggie, don't hide from your feelings."

"I—" Damn. Caught. I placed my hand on his and squeezed. "I'll meet you at the station, okay? We can talk after. This is just a little much right now."

His jaw tightened. He gave one short nod and climbed from the car.

Kissing his cheek and leaving the blanket on the cruiser's seat, Ginger and I ran for my vehicle. I cranked my heater and we maneuvered our way from the cul-de-sac. Multiple police cars, lined up behind each other like dominoes surprised me. The entire GFPD on-duty force must have hit the scene.

Ginger placed her hand on my arm. "Are you okay? Who'd believe Brad would flip out?"

Tears that had more to do with leaving Cam pooled in my eyes. I swallowed but my throat remained dry. "Did you hear what Brad said? Hurting me was nothing more than a "business decision.""

"And here we thought Cam would have to fight him off for your affections."

"Instead of just fighting him off." My thoughts

jerked me into remembering Cam struggling with an armed man.

"Maggie, do you want me to drive?"

"No, I'm fine."

"Uh, you may want to get back in your own lane before we leave this subdivision."

I pulled the car to the side and threw it into neutral. "You can drive. Thanks."

We maintained a desultory conversation, well, Ginger did, all the way to her house. She insisted on lending me clothes, and I put the towels she gave me to good use. Then we hit the police station. If I'd been driving, we may not have made all the stops.

Several hours later, my friends and I were huddled in the police station's main hallway. Cam joined us holding a tray of Java the Hutt to-go cups. As we sipped, a man whose appearance screamed "expensive lawyer" strode past, talking on a cell phone.

"My client agrees to a guilty plea on embezzlement charges with full restitution guaranteed." His voice faded as he moved away from our group. "Not guilty on the attempted murder charge."

The last words we heard were, "He's a CFO not a murderer. Let's talk assault and battery."

We exchanged startled glances. Ginger spoke first. "Do you think that's Brad's lawyer? Already?"

Cam frowned. "Seems like too much a coincidence not to be his." He slipped his arm around my shoulders after I shivered.

"But embezzlement? Attempted murder?" Katie crossed her arms. "What about two murders? Does Brad really think he can get away with Clarice and Nicole's deaths?"

Ginger put her hand on Katie's arm. "Wait a minute. Embezzlement makes sense. We all wondered where Clarice got her consulting money. What if it came from Brad?"

She turned to me, her face animated. "Didn't you tell me Mrs. Sievers mentioned that Clarice dated her son, Sam, then dumped him? Maybe Brad picked up where Sam left off. What if they'd kept in touch?"

I pondered her questions. "Mrs. Sievers told me someone else had a crush on Clarice in high school. She didn't name anyone, but Brad fits the bill. Plus, Clarice and Brad doing business together make sense. I can't get my head around Nicole and Brad, though. She tortured him for years."

Cam chimed in. "She could have now just in a different way, say, blackmail."

The group quieted.

"That I get," Katie said. "Nicole had her dirty paws involved." She turned to Ginger. "And don't go pinching my arm. I'll speak ill of the dead if they deserve it, and if anyone needs the truth told, it's Nicole. Was Nicole. Whatever."

Ginger dropped her hand.

Katie huffed. "Nicole plus blackmail has a nice ring to it." She raised her hands as if she framed a scene. "I can see it carved into a tree with a heart around it."

"And I can see you at home." Dirk stopped in front of Katie. "Sitting on the couch watching a chick-flick."

Katie arched her neck and looked past Dirk toward the front door. "What, are you practicing your Invisible Man Halloween costume? Where did you come from?"

He pointed at a nearby door. "Right over there.

Listening to girl detective and friends horning in on someone else's business. As usual."

"We're talking together. A group of friends. Nothing more."

"Right." His sarcastic tone would have shredded my skin if he'd been addressing me. Luckily Katie could handle the heat.

Katie crossed her arms then switched to putting her hands on her hips. "Not that you'll listen to us. Even though we've known these people for years."

""These people" are criminals or victims. You sure you want to identify yourselves with them?"

I didn't see Dirk move, but now he impinged on Katie's space. "If so, I've got a comfy little cell for you."

They exchanged a long glance. "I'm sorry," Katie said. "I know you've been getting pressure." She caught her lower lip between her teeth and looked at him from under eyelashes. "I wanted to help."

"Don't play the tease with me. Not now."

Dirk shook his head at Cam. "I figured you for more sense than hanging with this crowd." His gesture encompassed our bedraggled group.

Cam's arm tightened around me. "I did what I thought necessary."

Dirk eyed Cam. "Yeah, I get that." He brushed his hands through his hair. "Doesn't make it right, but I understand."

He treated the rest of us to a glare. "Go home. All of you. You're done here."

Dirk turned back to Katie. "And you'd better be finished with your snooping stuff too." He stalked off, shaking his head and muttering.

Ginger's disappointed look toward Katie would have me cringing in shame. Katie is made of sterner stuff.

"What. I never promised Dirk I'd stop thinking when we got together."

Cam pulled me into a hug. "Want me to drive you home?"

I wrapped my arms around his waist and kissed him before pulling away. "My car is here. Plus I owe Ginger a ride home."

Katie grinned. "I'm giving Ginger a ride. Go with Cam."

His proximity reminded me of my declaration. That statement about my feelings, the ones I hadn't fully come to terms with, yet. "I need time, Cam."

Cam's eyes narrowed. I wouldn't back down.

His palm cupped my cheek. "I don't see the difficulty. Either you love me or you don't."

I shook my head. "Not the point. I've got a few things to sort out. Call me later?"

"Don't listen to her," Katie interrupted. "Go over there and park your butt on her porch until she comes to her senses."

Ginger attempted a pincer action on Katie's arm, but she moved out of reach.

"What. It's the truth. The last time I saw someone not understanding her feelings it was me, looking in a mirror."

Ginger's mouth dropped open. Katie ignored her and grabbed my shoulder. "Don't let what happened years ago with that jerk-face Travis spoil what you have now with Cam." She dropped her hand. "That's all I'm saying. I'm going home and putting my feet up. It's been a long day." Katie walked for the door, pulling an unresisting Ginger with her.

Cam put his hands on my shoulders. "Katie's right. I'm not the shit-face who put you off men. You're not the bitch who told me she loved me then eloped with another guy. We've made mistakes in the past, sure. But we're better now, right? We deserve our love."

My throat closed with his words. Once again, Cam nailed me to the wall. Emotions riding high, I couldn't—shouldn't—speak.

"Okay. I'll back off. But I'm pissed. I want to be with you. Comfort you. It's a real slap in the face, you driving off without me for the second time tonight."

Cam's lips found mine in a hot, too brief kiss. "You want alone time? Fine. I'll call." He backed away. "No, this time I'm leaving it to you. You call me when you're sure about us." He ran his hands over his hair. "I hope you call soon. I love you, but I can't save you from yourself."

I watched him turn and stride away, his arms moving with short, jerky chops.

Damn. I'd really done it this time.

I'm not sure how long I stood in the hallway, but it couldn't have been protracted. Rousing myself, I walked to my car, the rain-slicked pavement reflecting streetlights. We'd been in the police station for longer than I realized, and night had fallen. The rain stopped, but heavy clouds threatened, swirling across the sky. My nostrils identified the aroma of wet leaves and moist earth.

The storm had wiped out the August humidity and left a fresh breeze. On another night, I'd have found the weather invigorating. I wrapped my arms around myself for emotional comfort. My stomach gurgled in complaint, but I had no taste for food. Someone I knew, thought I'd known, attempted to kill me earlier today. Cam had left, and even though it'd been at my request, I regretted turning him away. I shook with chills. I knew without hesitation that I needed Cam. I'd call as soon as I reached home.

I almost didn't see the dark sedan parked in my drive. Or the man standing beside the vehicle. My pulse increased and I couldn't catch my breath. I fumbled for my phone. The car idled for a quick get-away.

Then I recognized the man's silhouette.

Travis moved away from the car, his face highlighted by my neighbor's porch light. I parked and walked toward him.

Travis held his arms open then let them drop. A strange expression flew across his face. "Maggie, are you all right?"

His face, my memories of our long friendship before it went bad, returned in a rush. "You won't believe my day. Brad. He threatened me with a gun." *And worse, I pushed Cam away.*

His jaw dropped. "Crosby? Really?" He placed his hands on my shoulders and gave me a quick shake. "Tell me."

My stomach growled. Suddenly my appetite returned. "Come in. Have you eaten? I think I have some soup in the fridge."

He followed me, taking my keys and unlocking the door when my shaking hands couldn't handle the task. Travis helped me don a hoodie he'd grabbed from the couch and ushered me into a kitchen chair.

"Tell me where everything is and I'll heat your

food while you warm up."

His complexion looked pasty, but then mine potentially matched his for pale. I sat quietly, while Travis heated my food. When he finally settled across from me, I ate just enough to quell my hunger pangs. Putting down my spoon, I related most of the story.

"We heard a lawyer that we think is Brad's talking plea bargain, but he didn't mention murder." I played with my spoon. "It doesn't make sense. Ginger thinks Brad worked with Clarice, so her death may be linked back to him. But why Nicole?"

"I don't know." He rubbed his neck. "Maybe she blackmailed him." His voice broke on the last word.

Did he have personal experience with Nicole and blackmail? My gaze rested on my cooling soup. Voice pitched low, I changed the conversation's direction. "Travis, I have a personal question."

He kept silent, and I took that as permission to ask. "Have you stayed in touch with Nicole? Since college, I mean?" They'd attended the same university, a fact that had tormented me for several years.

He didn't reply immediately, and then with a question rather than an answer. "What are you asking?"

I collected my thoughts. Looking up, I settled my gaze on Travis's bowed head. "At the dinner dance last Friday, you told Nicole to be careful or her investments would bite her butt. Right?"

He remained silent, head down.

"How did you know? About her business, I mean?"

Now his answer came fast, too fast, and he didn't catch my eye. "She told me when we caught up at Sloane's Tavern."

His tone set my neck hair on edge. Dolores had

been decked out for a good time when I'd seen her at the spa before finding Clarice. Nicole had made it obvious during her massage that she'd meant to collect a man before the night ended. Talking business? When Nicole could potentially drive another stake through my heart with Travis? Unlikely.

"What do you know, Travis, and how are you involved?" My voice had a hard edge.

"You're better off not knowing."

I waited, hoping that he'd cave.

Finally, he gazed directly at me. "Nicole introduced me to some high-level investors when I opened my own business."

I saw the answer in his eyes but didn't trust my interpretation. "You let her get you involved with criminals? Were you laundering money?" When he didn't answer, I huffed a sigh. "I can't believe you were that dumb. Or greedy."

His face reddened but he remained silent.

"Did you try stealing their money or did you lose it?"

His voice choked as he answered. "My investors...don't like mistakes."

"Oh, Travis." I gnawed my lower lip as I thought. My next question came out as more a statement. "That's why you told me to stay uninvolved. That big money played by different rules. You knew the murderer's identity all along."

He dropped his eyes.

I held my breath.

He shook his head. "No, but Nicole bragged that she planned taking over Clarice's consulting business. She said that she had some added incentive that would make the clients work with her. I thought those murders were committed by the same person. Related, but not to my deal with Nicole."

Another piece fell into place. Nicole blackmailed Brad. That must have bit his butt.

"Travis, why were Clarice and Nicole killed? You know, don't you?"

He'd moved to the window and stood looking into the night. "Nicole promised the investors an easy return on her latest subdivision. She told me her father got suspicious. Either he wanted a cut for his back room deals or he wanted no part of the money men. I'm not sure. She thought she could sweet talk her way out of trouble. I tried to caution her. Nicole's death was, I don't know, maybe the investors tying up loose ends."

"That doesn't make sense. Why wouldn't the investors, I'm assuming mob types, just hire an assassin to take her out? Why send her a note written on my paper? A note arranging the meeting that led to her death? And pointed to me as the murderer?"

He shrugged, still not meeting my eyes. "Don't know."

"Travis, you need to tell the police about the investors. They think Brad is the only lead to Nicole. Well, besides me."

A remembered scene flashed across my consciousness. Travis and Brad sitting together. In deep conversation. Holy Crapola. I spoke without heed.

"I saw you. With Brad. At the country club bar. You were both there at the time of Nicole's death. You know who murdered her. Tell me."

His body tensed. His head remained turned away from me. "I don't know what you're talking about,

Maggie."

"Travis, please tell me you didn't kill Nicole." My voice cracked halfway through the sentence. My stomach had so many knots, a part of me wondered how I'd inhaled enough air to speak.

Still avoiding me he said, "I didn't do it, Maggie."

"Say that in a way I can believe, Travis." Damn, I shouldn't have made that comment.

Travis turned from the window. He smiled, but only sadness showed. "I really wish you hadn't confronted me about Nicole's death. Now I have to make a decision."

Chapter Nineteen

God save me from men making business decisions.

Travis cracked his knuckles, just as he had before a big varsity game. For luck, he'd said then. I didn't feel lucky now. Especially after he pulled a gun from his sport coat pocket, holding it loosely at his side.

Damn. Why did ex-classmates keep pulling guns on me? Did I have some strange magnetic thing going on? Or were guns just too damn easy to buy and license? I shook off the useless thoughts and focused.

"I didn't kill Nicole. Really. Don't ask me for explanations."

My thoughts raced. That meant Travis knew who'd killed her. Did he fear for his life?

"The problem is that now you know about Nicole's and my involvement with a felony. Two felonies."

"Yes, but not identities. Go to the police. They'll protect you."

"I don't intend on serving prison time." He shook his head. "She lied. Nicole lied about everything. She couldn't be trusted. You understand, right?"

I swallowed hard. His last words almost sounded like an excuse for murder. "Right." I inhaled but oxygen escaped me.

"Look, Travis, you haven't done anything wrong. Well, you have, but this can be fixed."

He shook his head. "Do you think I haven't looked

for an answer? I shouldn't be here, but I had to see you before I left. Should have realized you'd ask questions."

I blinked. Did he plan shooting me before he walked out? "You're leaving?"

"I promised my investors a full return of their money. With interest. In exchange, they agreed to let me live." He laughed. "That sounded like lines from a bad movie."

He glanced out the window. "Unfortunately, I decided that I couldn't afford their interest rates." Travis looked at the gun as if it were an interesting artifact. "I contacted the feds. I'm going into Witness Protection."

"So why do you have the gun, Travis? You're scaring the crap out of me." I inhaled through my nose. "Do you even know how to use that thing?"

"I thought I saw someone sneaking through your yard." He checked outside then moved closer. His eyebrows rose. "Yes, I know how to shoot. I've been carrying this since Nicole's murder. Then the Fed I worked with broke contact yesterday. In his last message he said to trust no one."

He caught my gaze. "But I've always trusted you. Well, except for when we broke up. That's why I stopped tonight." He cleared his throat. "I want the truth between us before I leave. You know we can never be in contact again."

My thoughts flew like birds in a disrupted aviary, but I recognized the chance to heal old wounds and grabbed it. "Why did you dump me for Nicole?"

"Nicole told me you were no virgin, your innocent act a ploy."

"I didn't lie to you, Travis."

"I know. I should have believed you then."

"I felt an emotional weight lift, along with a sense of completion. "Thank you." I rubbed my chest. "Just, you know, thanks."

Travis looked thoughtful. "I know this will sound crass but whoever killed Nicole did the world a favor." Our gazes met. "I'm just sorry we split up all those years ago. My life, well, I probably wouldn't be carrying a gun watching out the window for bad guys right now."

I found a grin and slapped it on my face. "At least not a gun made of steel."

His face lit up then he kissed my forehead. "I'd tell you to call me when you dump the youngster, but you won't have my number."

He walked to the door and turned. "Just so you know, I'd never have let you be convicted of murder."

"How were you planning to prevent that from happening?"

He frowned and moved to the side.

Then the glass window in my door exploded. Travis's body spun once before collapsing. I sat frozen for a moment. Common sense sent me out of the chair, crouching alongside the kitchen cabinets.

A preternatural quiet had fallen.

Grabbing a chair by its legs, I used it to sweep my handbag from the counter to the floor. The chair tipped and caught my ribs before falling to the side. Ignoring the flash of pain, I located my phone and called 9-1-1.

"Travis? Travis, are you okay?" The continued silence convinced me he needed help.

Grabbing a scatter rug from in front of the stove, I threw it over the broken glass and splinters. Loud crunches sounded when I crawled over the mess. I finally reached his side. He had a hole in his shoulder leaking a stream of blood. I pulled a wad of tissue out of my pocket and applied pressure over the wound.

"Stay with me, Travis. Come on, open your eyes. Let me see you're conscious." The tissues soaked through in seconds. Holding the pressure with one hand, I struggled out of my hoodie and added the jersey compress.

I heard my harsh breaths and whimpers and knew fear had taken over. Forcing a big breath, I concentrated on the emergency rather than my nerves.

"Hey, guy, don't screw with my special memory by dying."

Travis's eyelashes fluttered. Before I knew whether he'd regained consciousness, I'd been moved aside by a pair of EMTs. Working with practiced speed, they had Travis on a gurney and out the door before I caught my breath.

"Ms. Stewart?"

I struggled to focus, finally sighting in on a GFPD patrolman standing above me with his hand out. Placing my bloodied paw in his, I stood on wobbly legs. He wrapped me in a blanket and helped me to a chair.

Another set of EMTs crouched before me. I tried pushing them away. "No, check on Travis. He's shot." I choked on a breath. "Someone shot him. He may die."

One of the EMTs, a woman, put her hand on my shoulder. In a low, calming voice, she said, "Don't worry, Ms. Stewart. Your friend should be at the hospital by now."

My hands were covered with blood. The activity around me seemed fuzzy, and I couldn't stop shivering.

I heard just bits and pieces of the conversations swirling around me.

"Shock."

"One blanket's not gonna be enough."

"Quick, hand me the afghan."

I felt warm arms around me then I was wrapped in the familiar scents and textures of my heavy cotton blanket and wool afghan. I struggled to push the afghan off me. "Grannie's afghan. No blood."

The female technician put her mouth at my ear. "Don't worry. We'll make sure your afghan stays clean."

Those were the last words I heard until I woke up in a hospital bed.

****

"She's coming around," Ginger said.

"It's about time."

I smiled when I recognized Katie's gruff voice, the one she put on when she didn't want people to know she cared. No one had let on her subterfuge never worked.

"Hi." My voice sounded weak and rusty. I cranked up my eyelids.

"Hi yourself, Miss Shoot 'Em Up."

Ginger held a glass of water for me. After I sipped on a straw, I croaked out one word. "Travis?"

"Stable." Katie cleared her throat. "Doctor said he should recover fully."

"When can I go home?"

My friends exchanged glances.

Ginger answered. "Tonight, your doctor said. Unless you exhibit complications, but the only injuries they found were some deep cuts and assorted bruises."

She smoothed her hand over the blanket covering my arm.

"We thought you might like to stay with me tonight."

Oh. That's right. First work, then my house became a crime scene. Would I ever be rid of the yellow and black tape?

"Unless you want to stay somewhere else." Katie's voice held a hint I couldn't identify.

"I don't want to be a bother. I'll get a motel room."

Ginger sniffed. "Not on our watch, you won't." She put her hand on my shoulder. "Sweetie, you can live in pajamas, but you shouldn't get your bandages wet.

"Bandages?" When I couldn't wiggle my fingers, I pulled one hand out from under the covers. Gauzy material enclosed my hand.

Katie nodded. "Splinters in both hands. Glass cuts on your knees. Bruised ribs. Doctor said you'll be fine in a couple of days."

I shivered in remembrance until my ribs protested.

"Don't worry about your backdoor," Katie added. "Jim sent someone over. It's already fixed."

The destroyed back door didn't worry me. How I'd feel living in the house did.

A gray haired nurse entered. "Time to leave, ladies."

"Already?" Katie said. "We haven't had our ten minutes yet."

"Don't push me, sister. You're lucky you got in at all."

"We're family," Katie answered.

"Yeah, that's what the blond haired cutie in the hall

is claiming. He's been crawling all over the nurse's station, trying to get information." She sniffed. "Not that those young things did anything but bat their eyelashes."

My heart lifted. "Cam?"

The nurse pursed her lips. "That's the name. Any relation?"

"He's my—" My what? "Um, could I see him?"

"Only if these two get out of here. You don't need a party, not if you want the doctor releasing you today."

My friends patted my arms and hustled out. After a quick vitals check, the nurse left.

I watched the door, my pulse pounding in my ears. Cam cared. But given our last conversation, maybe he checked on me out of politeness. His words had hit my solar plexus and left me empty. I didn't want to feel that emotionally barren ever again.

Besides that, I wondered how he'd view the shooting I'd been in with Travis. And how I'd explain Travis's presence in my home. Would Cam trust my explanation?

Cam pushed through the door and stood just inside the entrance. "Hiya." His uncertain expression tore at my heart.

"Hiya." I waved a sheathed paw in his direction.

He moved closer and stood, shuffling his feet.

"I'm sorry."

Our simultaneous apologies startled me. "You? You have nothing to apologize about. Me." I caught my breath. "I'm the one in the wrong." My bandaged hand hovered above his.

He gently placed my hand on the bed. "I pressured you when you were already stressed." He rubbed the back of his neck. "But damn, Maggie. I could have lost you. That's all I could think of when I saw that shit-head squeezing the life out of you."

Cam dropped his head. His shoulders shook for a moment.

I raised my bed. "Cam."

He caught my gaze. His shiny eyes matched my own.

"The doctor says I can go home tonight."

He nodded.

"Ginger offered me a bed."

He looked like he wanted to protest then touched my cheek. "You'll be safe there."

"I know, but I'd rather not bother her." I cleared my throat. "I'd rather stay with you. That is, if you'll have me."

He cocked his head. "What did you say?" Cam's hand shot forward. He put two fingers over my mouth. "No, I heard you." He inhaled through his nose. "Yes. Stay with me."

"Are you sure you want to take on an invalid? You've got work and—"

"And I'll take a few days off. No problem." He kissed my forehead. "You know I want to take care of you forever, right?"

His husky voice caused tears to form. "Yeah, I know."

"So can I get a kiss before that drill sergeant nurse returns and kicks me out?"

I grinned. "What do you think?"

He swooped in, stopping with his lips hovering over mine. "No pressure, but I love you."

My room door swept open and my nurse stood tall,

checking her watch.

His kiss was short but sweeter than any of Mona's confections. He straightened.

"See you later. Have the nurse call me. I'll be in the waiting room down the hall." Cam grinned. "After we get home, I'll rent some chick flicks for you."

"Perfect." I swallowed. "I think the action movies are on hold for a while."

He ran the backs of his fingers across my uninjured cheek. "I love you."

My vision swam as I smiled back. "I love you too."

Chapter Twenty

The scents of Java the Hutt coffee and fresh baked cookies tempted my nose and stomach the next afternoon. Katie and Ginger had arrived at Cam's door minutes ago. He'd tucked me in on the couch, grabbed his keys and said he'd be back later.

They'd thoughtfully ordered iced coffees so I could use a straw. My bandages had been changed early this morning, and the doc found no signs of infection. I'd be back to work in no time.

"So how's Cam?" Katie's casual tone didn't fool me. She wanted information.

"He's fine. Dirk?"

"Satisfied."

Ginger leaned forward. "I don't mean to interrupt this scintillating conversation, but inquiring minds need to know. Katie, what did you get out of Dirk?"

I pointed at Katie. "Besides a love bite on your neck."

She slapped a hand to the very spot I'd noticed. "Damn him. I warned him to stop that high school crap."

Ginger and I laughed.

"C'mon, out with it." Ginger said it before I could, but that didn't lessen my interest.

Katie wiggled deeper into Cam's recliner. "Okay, but before I tell you anything, I need your promise you'll keep this information quiet."

Ginger and I raised our hands in what I'd recently learned comprised the Demonic Duo, now T-Cube secret gesture. "We promise."

I laughed with hitched breaths, wrapping my arm around my sore ribs. "So, how long do you think it'll be before everyone in town knows what you're about to tell us?"

"I figure one hour, end of the day tops."

"Well, then," Ginger said, "you'd better tell us fast. We don't want to hear this stuff second-hand."

Katie rubbed her hands. "You got it." She tapped her finger against her jaw. "Let's see. Where should I start?"

Ginger pursed her lips. "How about soon?"

"Okay, okay, sheesh. It's just that there's a lot of information, and I don't want to forget anything."

We looked at her. I knew Ginger's expression echoed my disbelief.

"Brad's confessed to Clarice's death. Says it was an accident. He denies killing Nicole."

"That aired on the morning news," Ginger scoffed. "Tell us something we can't get from television."

"Did he say how he got in my massage room?" The why I knew.

Katie shook her head. "He's lawyered up. No details forthcoming." I knew she likely quoted Dirk. "He did say he slipped out the window and closed it behind him.

"This next didn't make the morning news." Katie paused, making us wait a beat. "Brad said he paid Clarice as a consultant, filing phony invoices with his company." She sipped her coffee. "What Dirk didn't tell me, but Ginger figures, is that Brad used insider information and Clarice invested for him, getting a percentage of the profits."

Ginger picked up the story. "Rob told me he'd heard that the fight between BCI's CEO and Brad had to do with under-reporting profits. They were working on a merger. The CEO recently announced an outside auditor had been hired." She caught my eye. "Rob said that if Brad faked the financials or embezzled, he'd be in deep trouble."

"So that's what caused his panic. Because his mom overheard him demanding his money from Clarice."

"And she planned a long trip to Europe, remember?" I tapped my teeth with my fingernail. "So did Clarice plan to make off with Brad's money? Is that why he killed her?" I shook my head. "That doesn't make sense, because then he'd never get his money back."

"You're right." Katie sipped her coffee. "Dirk didn't say, but he mentioned that things often go wrong when people are desperate." She rubbed her forehead with her finger. "I think the auditor will find that Brad siphoned company money. Even if he replaced the funds out of his own accounts later, an ace auditor will find a trail."

Ginger snapped her fingers. "You know, that makes sense. I'll ask around, but I'll bet Clarice began her *consulting job* about the same time that Brad and his boss started fighting. Rob said Brad had been personally credited with their move to becoming a big player in the industry. Brad's the kind of guy who'd want something in return for the work he put into helping build BCI."

I sat forward. "Ginger is right. Brad wanted to make an impression at the reunion. To convince all of us that he wasn't a loser. That's why he dressed so well and bragged about his job." I thought for a moment. "And he offered the reward for information not only to look generous but to move suspicion from himself."

Katie nodded. "And you'd be right. Give the lady another cookie." She grabbed one for herself before holding the plate for me.

I took a cookie and bit down. Chocolate chip. Recovery should always be so sweet. "What about Nicole's business? Have they found the investors Travis mentioned?"

"Actually, the feds have stepped in citing RICO. Apparently Travis, via Nicole, tangled with some people who have been under investigation for a long time. Dirk thinks they knew Travis had contacted the feds and sent a shooter." Katie snorted. "Not to mention it's common knowledge our mayor can't be trusted to allow an unimpeded investigation. The State or the feds would have been called in sooner or later."

She wiped her fingers on a napkin. "Rumors flew that the mayor had a finger in Nicole's subdivision business. Stories about zoning permits issued without environmental impact studies were making the rounds."

I thought back to the subdivision site. "That subdivision we were in abuts wetlands, doesn't it?"

"Yeah, a creek runs through those acres. I remember my boss, Jim, commenting on that during one of our meetings." Katie's lips pursed. "The surrounding roads couldn't support the additional traffic, either."

"Dirk thinks the feds will file kickback and fraud

charges against the mayor once they find proof."

"Travis told me he planned on turning state's evidence. Is he following through?"

Katie and Ginger exchanged glances.

"He's already in a safe location. We won't see him again."

We allowed that statement to die without further discussion. I wondered how long it'd take before for my last view of his bloody body faded. A long time, I reckoned.

I knew I'd never believe in his innocence again. Human nature had provided me with a steep learning curve, and I wouldn't doubt my hard-earned lessons, not even for old friends.

I broke the silence. "That's an awful lot of crime for Granville Falls. You'd think we had the Dixie Mafia working out of our downtown. And almost all the members came from our graduating class."

Katie choked on cookie crumbs. Ginger jumped to pat her on the back, but she held up her hand. "You got that right," she gasped.

"And what about the note written on my note pad?" I glanced between my friends. "I'm still not off the hook for Nicole's murder, am I."

"Matt let something slip to me earlier today," Ginger said.

"Matt?" Katie's eyebrows rose. "Does this mean you're finally ready to give Rob the heave-ho he deserves?"

Ginger's lips tightened. "This is about Maggie, not me."

Katie's smile told us she wouldn't let Ginger off so easily, but she'd bide her time.

"Brad admitted grabbing one of your note pads just in case he needed it." Ginger covered my hand with hers. "I'm sorry, Maggie, but he said a good CFO always plans ahead."

My eyes widened. "He planned it? He meant to frame me?"

"Actually, yes and no. He acknowledged writing Nicole the note but he says they'd met by accident earlier that day and had already settled their business. He claims he didn't know Nicole kept the note."

I tried sitting then winced and reclined. "What a crock. Brad sent that note, kept the appointment, killed Nicole then ran. He'd planned it knowing the wait staff would be concentrated on serving. With only desserts in the walk-in, no one would discover the body until after he'd left."

"Took calculated nerve," Katie said. "But Dirk will nail him, I guarantee."

Ginger squeezed my hand. "Brad's lawyer is going for involuntary manslaughter with Clarice. He's been telling the press he thinks Brad never meant to kill her."

"Does he think a jury will believe she slipped and fell on my massage table after Brad accidentally pushed her during an argument?"

Ginger shrugged. "Who knows what story he'll cook up? He's got some time, and his lawyer will be spinning the story all through the trial."

"That's why he's not copping to Nicole," Katie added. "Even if he's convicted, involuntary manslaughter is a lesser charge than premeditated murder." She grinned. "Too bad his nefarious plan won't work, because you can place him at Nicole's murder scene. Well, mostly there. In the same building.

At the right time."

"Yes, it's a good thing you remembered seeing Brad and Travis in the cocktail lounge," Ginger said. "Matt told me the bartender has verified that Brad had a drink there right before Nicole's body was discovered."

"Besides, other people than you have better motive for killing Nicole," Katie explained holding up one finger. She added another finger. "Your means and opportunity are shaky or non-existent." A third finger popped up. "Scene evidence finally came back proving you weren't in that refrigerator. No footprints." She grinned. "Well, mine were there but not yours."

"I spoke with Tom Jenkins earlier this morning," Ginger said. "He's already issued a press release. Everyone in town watching television news reports will know you are innocent of Nicole's murder."

"Heck," Katie sniffed. "They'll know before then. Osmosis, I swear." She sipped her coffee. "Your testimony, the written note, along with the footprints they're working to isolate, will put Brad away for a long time. Plus, the fact that no knives were missing from the country club points to premeditation. And that's only part of the story."

I blew a long breath, my chest feeling lighter than it had for days. Not only had I escaped a murder indictment, I'd come to terms with a past that had held me back. And kept my massage business, besides. Nicole would hate having helped me out. No matter where she'd ended up though, I knew the pain she'd put me through didn't matter any longer.

"Right before his shooting, Travis told me he'd have made sure I didn't get convicted of Nicole's murder." I caught the gaze of my friends in turn. "Do you think Travis is capable of murder?" I knew what I thought, and I didn't like the answer.

Ginger pursed her lips. "We weren't there, we can't know what happened. Let's remember friends the way they were."

"Put your minds at rest," Katie said. "That's the final news I have. Dirk said I could tell you because a press release will be issued later this afternoon."

We huddled together, even though we were in Cam's house and no one could hear us.

Katie continued. "Travis made a full statement before leaving with the feds. He fingered Brad for both murders, in exchange for not getting hit with an accessory after the fact charge. Apparently, Travis taped Brad. Brad not only admitted killing both women, he threatened Travis with the same end."

"So that's how Travis planned to prove my innocence." I felt a full inhalation enter my lungs for the first time in days, then my temper rose. "But why hadn't he stepped forward earlier instead of leaving me hanging?"

Ginger rubbed my blanketed foot in sympathy. "I expect it had something to do with the mob types. Travis had to secure his own future before he could help you."

Katie snorted. "That sounds like Travis, all right."

"He lied to me. Right before he was shot, he told me he didn't know the murderer's identity." I shook my head. "It's a good thing he's out of reach."

"I feel sorry for Mrs. Crosby."

"She'll probably leave town," Katie said.

"Too bad," Ginger said. "She has friends here. Talk will die down."

I knew the healing power of friends, but figured Katie had her situation pegged. Gossip would send Mrs. Crosby looking for a new life. We leaned back, sipped our drinks, and munched cookies.

"I'd say there are so many loose ends to all this, we'll be wading through the crap for months." Katie gave a satisfied smile. "Including electing a new mayor."

I understood her pleasure. The mayor had publicly been on Dirk's back more than once after Nicole's murder. Seeing Mayor Polk leave office would give Katie the best gift she'd had since Dirk entered her life. In fact, Katie would probably drop off packing boxes at City Hall on her way home. That's what I loved about her. She could twist the knife when needed.

Thank goodness she was on my side.

"I'll tell you one thing," Ginger said.

Katie countered. "What's that?"

"I'm withdrawing my name from the twentieth class reunion planning committee. No way I want anything to do with that event."

Katie and I looked at each other and visibly shivered.

"Girlfriend," Katie said, "I'm with you."

Chapter Twenty-One

Cam and I were enjoying an Indian summer day picnic. Deep Carolina blue skies were punctuated with wispy white clouds. Sporadic leaf color covered the hills. The sun's heat lessened the effect of the nippy breeze that helped make the day comfortably beautiful.

We lay beside each other on a plaid wool blanket, our shoulders touching. A glass jar with fall flowers was tucked into a corner of the picnic basket. Besides the flowers, a selection of delicacies from the upscale market, and Mona's chocolates, Cam had surprised me with a bottle of my favorite wine. I was thirsty but too lazy to refill our glasses.

I tipped my head back to catch the sun and pondered how my life had changed. The sensation of lying under a guillotine had disappeared.

My massage business had hit a new high, featuring an almost full regular schedule with steady clients. I hoped the notoriety had less to do with my business uptick than my massage skills. After all, if I couldn't massage my way out of a paper bag, they'd stop coming. The publicity surrounding the murders hadn't hurt though.

Many of my new patrons were from the country club set, so in one sense, I had Nicole to thank. I hoped she'd finally found peace. After I'd had time for thought, I recognized Nicole had led a troubled life. She deserved release. She'd sure been a better friend than anyone knew.

Nicole had left her entire estate to Dolores. Her will declared Dolores a "faithful friend." Gossip had run rampant about her leaving her estate to a friend rather than her father. I wasn't surprised. Dolores had cried then opened a bottle of champagne in Nicole's memory. I'd even had a sip. Just seemed right.

My thoughts continued wandering as I absorbed nature's heat. I roused myself and asked Cam's input when I couldn't get past a worry.

"Cam, do you think Ginger had anything to do with Tom Jenkins taking my case on as pro bono?"

He stirred and rolled onto his side. "Nope. I think he told you the truth. You faced down two felons, helped save a man's life, and along the way fed him information that his investigator could use to prove your innocence. You put more work into your case than he did."

"Ginger said Tom returned her retainer. Do you think that's true? I'd hate to owe her money."

Cam selected a flower from the jar and brushed it over my cheekbone. "She wouldn't lie to you, Mags."

"Maybe I'll send him a gift certificate for a free massage. Do you think he'd like that?"

He leaned over, his head blocking the sun from my eyes. "I would." He kissed me. "Yeah, I think that'd be nice."

That decision sat well with my conscience and my sun-warmed body. "Good."

I figured the day just couldn't get any better. I was wrong.

Cam straightened and rubbed his neck with one

hand. "You know, the last time I did this, I almost posted my question on an advertising billboard over on I-40." Cam smacked his forehead with his palm. "Damn it. I shouldn't have said that. I'm sorry. I don't know why that statement came out of my mouth."

I sat up blinking. Cam's words about a billboard had my heart pumping like I'd just walked out of a too-hot sauna. Katie had related Cam's story when he and I began dating. Not that everyone in town hadn't already known about his proposal and failed engagement in detail. An electronic billboard featured as part of the proposal story.

He faced me. His serious mien scared me while sending excited tingles down my spine.

He took my hands in his. "Mags, you know I love you."

I nodded, too shaken for words.

"You know I'd do anything for you." He licked his lips and cleared his throat. "I want you with me." He squeezed my hands. "Always."

"Cam," my voice broke. "I don't—"

"You don't what? Love me?" He leaned away, my hands still enfolded in his. His pupils darkened. "I know you do."

My gaze searched his face. I knew I loved him to distraction. If nothing else had come from my brush with murder, I had that awareness. Cam would always be the love of my life. But what about when my body sagged and he still had almost seven years of youth more than mine? Could I keep his interest or would he leave me when life got serious?

Like the other male who had? No, not Cam.

Because he knew me better than anyone, he

answered my unspoken apprehension. "I won't get tired of you. I don't see our age difference as meaning anything at all. I love you. I will always love you. Through thick and thin. Murderers included."

My lips kicked up a smile at his last phrase. His hands relaxed his grip when he noticed. "Besides, you've been living with me for almost a month. We may as well make a perfect situation permanent."

That's Cam. Practical to the nth degree. And in a hurry I didn't totally share.

"You're mine, Mags. And I'm yours." He dropped my hands and reached into his shirt pocket. He enfolded a small object in my right palm. "Marry me?"

I opened my hand. A ring sporting an emerald surrounded with small diamonds glittered there. My breath took a hiatus and my heart beat triple time.

"To match your eyes." His Adam's apple moved. "The emerald, I mean."

I couldn't help myself. I smiled. "I figured that's what you meant."

Cam wasn't just practical.

"So? What do you think? I'm in this, us, for the long haul."

Decision time. Either I trusted his love or I didn't.

Nerves had pulled the skin taut over his high cheekbones. His face held a light blush and his blue eyes looked black with desire. He swallowed.

Almost as a reflex, I swallowed too. Then I licked my dry lips. Our gazes met and held.

"I can't think of anything I'd like more."

Giddiness competed with certainty when he lifted the ring from my palm and gently placed it on my left hand. Tears gathered in my eyes.

"Woo-hoo!" Cam's voice seemed to echo around me, or it could be that he'd yelled in my ear. Either way, his exuberance made me laugh.

We kissed for what seemed like hours, but couldn't have been long. When we broke apart, the sun still hit me at the same degree as it had before.

"When I bought the wine, I hoped we could use it for a toast."

"Then let's get to it."

Cam poured wine into both glasses and handed me one. "To us."

I echoed his words and we tapped rims, the crystal ringing true. Yes, he'd outfitted the basket with crystal, china, linen, and the aforementioned flowers. If I hadn't already known he was all man, I might have worried. He caressed my cheek with his fingers. "So, let's not have a long engagement, okay? Thanksgiving is my favorite holiday. Let's get married then."

This decision would change my life for the rest of my years. Although I knew I'd made the best—the only—choice agreeing to marry Cam, I still needed some processing time. My thoughts whirled. Engaged. Who'd have thought? Not me, that's for sure.

I held back more out of habit rather than lack of desire. "Thanksgiving? That's only two months away. Don't you think that's kind of soon? Unless you mean Thanksgiving next year? That would be better." I cleared my throat and ended my babbling.

"Am I pressuring you?"

I turned that idea over for a moment. "No, you're not. I wouldn't have said yes if I didn't want you, us. It's just that you may change your mind. Maybe we should keep this to ourselves for a while."

The ring, now decorating my left hand, caught both our attention.

He captured my gaze. "I think keeping anything to ourselves in this town is impossible." He pushed a lock of hair behind my ear. His voice rang low and deep. "I won't change my mind, Maggie. That's you being scared, not my truth."

I believed him, but another fear broke free. That had to be the reason I kept throwing up roadblocks to commitment. "I haven't even met your family. What if your parents don't like me? I mean, I graduated school with your older brother for cripes sake." I cleared my throat again. "It's a good thing your brother was out of town on business during the reunion weekend. That would have been too strange."

Cam kissed me. "I don't give a rat's ass what they think, but I know they'll be happy because I love you."

I pulled from his embrace. "Yes, what your family thinks does matter. We can't build a life if the people you love most won't talk to us. What about holiday dinners?"

His thumb rubbed over my lips. "Holiday dinners aren't the point. My family loves me, warts and all. All it'll take is one look at us together and they'll know what you mean to me. Any other excuses? 'Cause I want to start celebrating."

Dread waited, coiled within me like a sleeping snake. But Cam waited for my answer. We could work this out another time. I shook my head.

"Good, enough said." He kissed me again, hotter this time, demanding. "Let me show you how I feel about you. Just in case you've forgotten."

Laying me flat out on the blanket, he covered me

partially with his weight. His erection pressed against my lower half in just the right way. My juices flowed.

Cam nipped my earlobe. His teeth scraped the soft area behind my ear. "Feel what I mean? It's all yours, Megs."

He made an excellent case on his own behalf. "I see your point."

His lips moved across my temple to lightly kiss my eyelids. His head blocked the sun, and I opened my eyes to gaze into his darkened pupils.

"However, I think I may need a more persuasive argument."

He smiled. "I'm just getting started."

Cam made a controlled roll to his back, keeping me in his arms. Bracing my hands on the rough blanket, I felt the warm sun along my spine. The aroma of crushed leaves and dried grasses rose to my nostrils.

One hand caressed the nape of my neck, while the other teased my nipple between his fingers. Heat unconnected to solar power shot through my body. I heard panting. My own with a bass accompaniment from Cam.

I ran a finger across his eyebrow. "You can be very convincing."

We exchanged hot, wet, open-mouthed kisses.

His breath sawed unevenly. "I'm glad you said that. Let me show you more." His hips rose from the blanket. "Just in case you still have doubts."

I let my doubts go hang themselves.

****

Katie's lips straightened. "A cape is a unique fashion statement."

Ginger raised an eyebrow. "A black vinyl cape at a

wedding is not a fashion statement, it's a disaster. Especially considering where that thing has been before." She pursed her lips. "Besides, Maggie doesn't need our version of a good luck charm." She looked me over. "New, old, borrowed, blue, all in place. Check."

"I've told you before," Katie said. "This cape is a collectible. Hey, you could fold and wrap my cape around her waist. No one would notice."

"Are you nuts? Don't bother answering that, Katie. I asked a rhetorical question."

I tuned out their squabbles designed I knew, to lessen my wedding day nerves. Katie and Ginger didn't believe me when I told them I had no dry throat or upset stomach. No adrenaline spiked my veins. Calm assurance flowed through my bloodstream.

I don't remember the exact moment I'd accepted and forgiven the past. A specific date and time didn't matter. Facing the future with the man I loved? That's what counted. We'd already committed to each other. The show today, well, my mom would've loved it.

Cam's family rallied and helped us pull together our wedding. I hadn't known I craved a warm family atmosphere until I'd walked into his parents' house for the first time. His siblings and their kids had been there, and my stomach cramped when I saw my old classmate, Red Darrow. He joked about his kid brother getting lucky and scoring the woman his teen-aged self had wanted. We all laughed, including Red's wife.

Then he said it didn't matter which Darrow I married as long as I joined their family. That's when I stopped worrying about his family's support. As Cam said, we didn't need their okay, but I felt better.

Ginger's hand on my shoulder interrupted my

thoughts, bringing my attention back to the room.

"It's time."

We swept from the room in our last official appearance as the T-Cubes, although without Katie's cape. Marrying Cam made amulets superfluous. As far as crime fighting went, well, I still couldn't bring myself to watch mysteries, much less action movies. I'd leave that excitement to Katie and Ginger.

Katie whispered in my ear. "Cam's one lucky guy. Be sure he shows you what the guys at work bought him for your honeymoon." She smiled.

A momentary flicker of worry fluttered in my stomach. Aw, heck, I'd faced more than a construction gang's gag gift and come out the winner. Instead, I walked in to the small church's foyer the day before Thanksgiving wearing an ear-to-ear grin.

Even though I swore my nerves were unaffected, the procession and minister's short sermon passed in a blur. I didn't register sights or sounds besides Cam from the moment I saw him waiting for me. Until the time to repeat the vows we'd written arrived. Each word filled my consciousness and became etched on my heart.

After the declaration that we were joined in holy matrimony, Cam brought my hand to his lips and kissed each finger one by one. His gaze didn't leave mine. Then he lowered his head and brushed my lips with his.

His caress. I'd be grateful for his touch every day of my life.

Marriage. The best promise we'd made each other. So far.

A word about the author...

Ashantay Peters loves escaping into a well-written book. Her reading addiction also has her perusing magazines, newspapers, Internet articles, and even food labels. The last is usually feebly excused as an attempt to maintain health, however.

She lives in the mountains of western North Carolina, a happy transplant from the much colder (and flatter) Midwest. Gardening, reading, photography, and walking are her favorite activities.

Please contact her at ashantay.peters@gmail.com or check out her website: www.ashantay.com. Be sure to ask her about her progress on her next book, *Death Crop*.

~*~

Other Ashantay Peters titles
available from The Wild Rose Press, Inc.:

DEATH STRETCH
DEATH UNDER THE MISTLETOE